The backyard light came on, evident through the toile curtains that hung halfway down the kitchen window.

Despite her nervousness, Melinda put aside her grandmother's journal and walked over to the door. Probably just some wayward raccoon or neighborhood cat, but it never hurt to check....

As she stood in the middle of the kitchen floor, the teapot started to whistle.

The figure of a large man loomed in the window of the kitchen door. Melinda screamed.

And then her brain registered what her eyes saw.

"Nicholas!" His name was a strange mix of strangled cry and whispered prayer. Before her feet could respond to her brain's order to move, Nick had unlocked the door and it swung open.

> "Geri Krotow's assured debut is a true gift
> to readers—a novel packed with emotion
> and filled with an expansiveness that crosses
> generations. It combines a woman's journey
> of the heart with her discovery of devastating
> secrets of the past, all adding up to a
> triumphant and uplifting conclusion."
> —Susan Wiggs, *New York Times* bestselling author

Dear Reader,

This story will always be special to me not just because it's my first published novel, but because it's the story of Esmée and Jack, two souls deeply committed to the cause of freedom during World War II. Their courage and stamina allowed them to survive their numerous trials during the war—and to fall in love and have a family to carry on their rich legacy.

Esmée and Jack represent so many people who did what was right and just, regardless of the consequences. From occupied Belgium to a life in the United States after the war, Esmée and Jack work through all the challenges most married couples do. Ask any couple who's been together for one or many decades; no one will tell you that marriage is easy. But it *is* possible, and worth any struggle when you know you're with the right partner.

Today we have many tools to help us through the tough spots—counselors, workshops, even talk shows can shed light on solutions for various problems. Esmée and Jack, and their generation, did not have all of this at their disposal. Yet they survived, and their love thrived, because it's an everlasting love.

Esmée and Jack's granddaughter Melinda and her husband, Nick, have become special to me, too, as they face what many of us face today. As spouses return to their families from war-torn areas, adjustments must be made. We have help now, and we have each other. We have love.

Thank you for choosing this story to read. I welcome your comments at www.gerikrotow.com or gerikrotow@gerikrotow.com.

Geri Krotow

A Rendezvous To Remember

GERI KROTOW

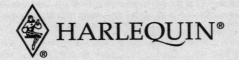

HARLEQUIN®

TORONTO • NEW YORK • LONDON
AMSTERDAM • PARIS • SYDNEY • HAMBURG
STOCKHOLM • ATHENS • TOKYO • MILAN • MADRID
PRAGUE • WARSAW • BUDAPEST • AUCKLAND

ISBN-13: 978-0-373-65422-2
ISBN-10:   0-373-65422-7

A RENDEZVOUS TO REMEMBER

This edition published by arrangement with Harlequin Books S.A.

® and TM are trademarks of the publisher. Trademarks indicated with
® are registered in the United States Patent and Trademark Office, the
Canadian Trade Marks Office and in other countries.

www.eHarlequin.com

Printed in U.S.A.

ABOUT THE AUTHOR

Raised in Buffalo and western New York State, Geri always dreamt of romance and adventure. A graduate of the U.S. Naval Academy, she moves around the world with her Navy pilot husband, two children, a dog and a parrot. Geri loves to hear from readers. You can reach her at www.gerikrotow.com.

Dedication

For Stephen
My Everlasting

Acknowledgment

My heartfelt gratitude, respect and love to
Haywood Smith, Susan Wiggs and Debbie Macomber
for believing in me and my potential. You are soul sisters.
Special thanks to my editor extraordinaire,
Paula Eykelhof.

Chapter 1

November 10, 2007

He stood hunched over the azaleas, shaping the bushes with ease despite the cold. Melinda Busher-Thompson burrowed her gloved hands deeper into the front pockets of her Berber coat as she watched him. Her exposed skin stung with the raw damp of the November day—another reason for her desire to leave western New York.

Yet Grandpa Jack moved through his garden as though he was still forty, like her, and not eighty-seven.

As if Grammy was still here.

"Hey, Grandpa." Her all-weather moccasins squished over the scattered dead leaves Grandpa Jack had laid down for insulation.

"Hey, yourself, kiddo!" Pleasure lit up Jack Busher's

face. Melinda caught the sparkle in his violet-blue eyes before he enfolded her in one of his famous bear hugs.

Grandpa Jack might be thinner than he'd been when she was a child, but his embrace still held all the love in the world for her. She breathed in his scent—fall morning rain mixed with soap and old-fashioned cologne.

"I didn't think you'd get here until tomorrow."

The familiar vestiges of his English accent comforted her.

Jack pulled back to look at Melinda's face but his hands were still on her upper arms. He squeezed her with just enough pressure that she felt it under her thick coat. Her heart pounded in response to the unconditional love she'd only ever found here with him and Grammy.

"I got into town late last night."

"I see." Jack grunted as he hoisted a pile of twigs he'd gathered and tossed them into his wheelbarrow.

"I didn't want to wake you." She held her breath for a moment, then watched the cloud of vapor as she expelled it forcefully from her lungs.

"I slept at my house last night but I have my luggage in the car so I can stay with you for the next two weeks."

Jack's expression stiffened.

"That won't work, honey. You belong in your own place."

"Grandpa, I belong with you right now."

She felt her neck muscles tighten in exasperation.

Grandpa refused to accept her broken marriage for what it was.

Irreparable.

"Melinda, you've always belonged with me, you'll always be part of me. But no one's been in your house for months, except me checking on it, and it needs some living. It'll do the place good to have the furnace on and water running through the pipes."

Jack paused in his raking and leveled a look at Melinda. It was the same look he used to give her as a teenager when he saw through her schemes.

"I'm not so old that I need a babysitter, honey."

"I'm not here to babysit you, Grandpa. I miss you and we'll have more time together if I stay here."

"Phooey. We'll have all the time we want. You need to be in your own home."

He wasn't going to back down on this one. Nor was he willing to discuss Nick with her.

Not yet.

"You taking care of yourself, girl?" Jack's body might be fading but his eyes and perception weren't.

"Sure, Grandpa." She glanced down, but felt the strength of his gaze. "It's not easy, you know...."

Her cheeks flushed with shame. How could she stand here whining about her loss when Grandpa mourned the loss of his life's partner of more than sixty years?

His breath caught, and she heard the rasp in his throat. When she raised her eyes back to his, she saw the unshed tears. Guilt and grief washed over her and she clenched her fists in her coat pockets.

"Of course it's not easy, pumpkin, but we have to go on. *We're* still here. You know your Grammy wouldn't have it any other way."

He bent down to pick up the shears he'd dropped at their feet. When he straightened, she saw the strain on his face.

"I know, Grandpa. I'm sorry. I'm being a bitch."

Jack's eyebrows rose. "Nothing this family hasn't experienced from its women before."

They both laughed, and for a moment all the sorrow of the past three months was gone and it was just Melinda and Grandpa Jack out in the garden.

Exactly the way it'd been since Melinda could remember. She'd even taken her first steps here. Busher family legend said she'd reached for a tulip to pick, unaware of the rarity of bulb flowers in a Buffalo spring.

"Honey, I called you for a reason." She heard the slight quaver in his voice, saw the deep lines around his mouth.

"Grandpa, you don't have to explain. I told you I'd come whenever you needed me, and I meant it. I'm just sorry I didn't come sooner."

The truth was, she'd had to convince Senator Hodges that she'd only be gone two weeks. Thank God it wasn't an election year or she'd never have gotten this vacation time. Since she'd taken over as head speechwriter for the senator, she'd had exactly one week off.

When Grammy died.

"You have your own life, Melinda. I don't expect you to drop everything for me. You know that, honey." He raked up the clippings from the azaleas and stooped to put them in the black plastic bag.

"Let me help you, Grandpa."

Together they finished the rest of the job, and within twenty minutes were inside the warm kitchen. The kitchen was home to Melinda ever since Grandpa and Grammy moved into the large suburban house in the 1970s.

Hot coffee steamed from Grammy's chipped ceramic mugs that Melinda set on the table in front of them.

"Your Grammy was always closest to you, Melinda, even more so than she was to your father or Lille." Jack's hands tightened around his mug.

"We don't have to talk about this, Grandpa." Sad conversations weren't good for Grandpa Jack. Not in his deep state of grief.

"Yes, my dear, we do. Now let me finish."

He covered Melinda's hand with his, and a lifetime of Grandpa Jack conversations flooded through her heart at the contact. Tears seeped from her eyes but she remained silent.

This isn't about you, Melinda. Be strong for Grandpa Jack.

"As close as Grammy was to you, my dear, she didn't share everything. *We* didn't share everything, not with anyone, really."

Melinda sucked in a breath. Now what? She was

going to find out she had long-lost sisters or brothers? The family had a fortune from bootlegging that they'd kept in Swiss accounts?

Grandpa Jack appeared oblivious to her thoughts.

"As you may remember, we married after the war, here in Buffalo." Grandpa Jack looked out the kitchen window and as much as Melinda wanted to follow his gaze, she couldn't stop staring at his face.

What was he going to tell her?

"But that's not where the story started. Your father was born in 1944." Melinda heard Grandpa's words but still didn't follow him.

"Yes, so he's sixty-three."

"And your aunt Lille's one year older than he is."

"Sixty-four." As she did the math, Melinda realized that Aunt Lille seemed much younger than her years. But surely this wasn't why Grandpa Jack was going through the family timelines.

"And your Grammy and I were married for—"

"Sixty-one years," Melinda finished for him.

Silence fell, and Grandpa Jack just watched her. She looked back at him, unsure of where he was headed with this. Okay, so there were a few years between her aunt's and father's births and Grammy and Grandpa Jack's wedding. That was hardly uncommon during World War II.

Wasn't he her biological grandfather? Was that the big secret?

"So you weren't Grammy's first husband?"

What kind of question was that? she asked herself. How much of a comfort was she to Grandpa Jack now?

Grandpa Jack showed no concern at Melinda's comment. He laughed.

"Oh, honey, no, that's not what I'm trying to tell you. Your Dad's my son, no question." But he didn't say anything about Aunt Lille.

Melinda knew she should've asked Grammy more about her life, especially after Grammy was diagnosed with cancer last year. But the final date of her divorce from Nicholas loomed, and overwhelmed by the thought of losing Grammy, it hadn't occurred to her.

She'd been too self-absorbed.

"So why the gap, Grandpa? It was the war, right?"

"I was in a concentration camp."

The words flew like bullets from a sleek pistol. Quiet. Oh, so smooth.

Shocking.

"But, Grandpa…why? Are you Jewish?"

Melinda had never seen any great religious fervor in Grandpa and Grammy. They were spiritual, and both their children, as well as Melinda, had been raised Catholic, but not in a strict way.

Melinda racked her brain, trying to remember everything she'd learned about concentration camps during World War II. She recalled that more than thirteen million had been slaughtered in the Holocaust. Six million Jews and the rest a mix of Catholics, Gypsies, homosexuals and whoever else didn't fit Hitler's grand scheme for the "master race."

She'd never seen any connections between her grandparents' lives and what she'd studied.

"No, honey," her grandfather answered. "I'm not Jewish, but your Grammy and I tried to help the Jews. We also worked against the Nazis when they moved into Belgium, and the rest of Northern Europe, for that matter."

Grandpa Jack's statements poured out of him as though he'd spoken of this his entire life.

But Melinda had never heard any of it before. All her grandparents had ever said about their lives prior to arriving in America was that "times were tough. We're happy to be together now."

Certainly their son, James, Melinda's father, had never revealed any knowledge of their past. He just said his parents were from Europe. Aunt Lille had never revealed that she knew anything, either.

"You're from England, and Grammy was from Belgium, right?"

"Yes, that's true. But it was unusual for a Brit to meet a Belgian like your grandmother during the middle years of the war. The circumstances we found ourselves in…"

Grandpa Jack's voice trailed off and he gazed down at the coffee in his cup. He took a swig.

After a moment he said, "Your grandmother kept a journal. Hell, more than a journal—it's our life together.

And her life before she met me. Our tough times, even after the war, here in America. It's part of your legacy, Melinda."

"Why didn't you mention this sooner?" Melinda searched her memory for all the times Grandpa Jack could've told her about Grammy's journal. For that matter, why hadn't Grammy said anything while she was alive?

"We've always been reluctant to talk about the war years." Jack grew still, his expression somber. "We experienced struggles that, until recently, would've been unimaginable to you, to your parents."

Melinda knew what he meant. Until September 11, 2001, most North Americans wouldn't have been able to fathom the depth of suffering experienced at the hands of the Gestapo in occupied Europe.

"There's one more thing, my dear. I kept a diary after my release from the concentration camp. I've never even shared it with Grammy. She'd already suffered too much by the time I found her again. But you deserve to know both sides of our story."

Grandpa Jack looked at her and raised his chin. Slightly, but enough for Melinda to read the pride and conviction on his face.

"We went through hell to get our freedom."

Chapter 2

The heavy, leather-bound journal sat on Melinda's lap. Pages jutted out from its frayed edges, added later or falling out from age. It was one of several books Grandpa Jack had given to her, all with Grammy's writing.

Melinda ran her hands over the dark brown cover, as though she could somehow sense Grammy's love, feel her presence.

God, she missed Grammy so much.

As an adult she should be past needing her grandmother's affection. Most of her friends and colleagues had lost their grandparents far sooner than she.

Yet the long talks and the hours spent cooking and baking together were all woven into the fabric of her life with Grammy. She just wanted to be able to pull out that blanket one last time.

A tear slipped from her eye and Melinda blinked.

She'd cried enough these past few years, hadn't she?

If not about Nicholas, then about Grammy.

Nicholas.

She glanced around the Victorian home they'd restored in the early years of their marriage. The floral wallpaper in the living room reminded her of her neglected rose garden, out back. She and Nicholas had made love there on more than one occasion, in the gazebo.

What had brought that memory to the surface?

She swiped at her tears. Maybe coming home to Buffalo hadn't been the best idea, after all.

But Grandpa had called. And Grammy's words called her now.

And no way was Grandpa going to let her stay with him.

Melinda pulled on the leather string that held the journal together. Despite the cracked condition of the book, the string ran soft and supple through her fingers. She whispered a quiet prayer, lifted the old leather cover…and saw a large cream envelope with her name written on it in Grammy's shaky cursive.

Melinda

The envelope was fairly new.

Grammy had left her one final birthday card, perhaps? She'd turned forty a week ago, and Grammy had always made it a point to celebrate Melinda's birthday. Even when she'd been on assignment in D.C. last year, Grammy had sent balloons and chocolate to her one-bedroom efficiency condo.

Melinda opened the envelope. The edge of the flap gave her a paper cut but she paid no heed.

This was no birthday card.

Grammy had left her a sympathy card. A white embossed dove rose from a pale blue background, and the words To Comfort You in Your Loss were written across the top in silver. Melinda read the message inside.

Dear Melinda,

This is a sympathy card because by now I figure you're missing me a lot. Know that I am with you and I'll always love you. As much as I'm confident that I'll be having a grand time wherever I am, know that I must somehow miss you, too. Unless, of course, I'm allowed to haunt you. In the most positive way, of course! No, I haven't lost my mind, I'm just losing my body and I wanted to write this before it's too late. Please read the enclosed letter before you start my journal.

XOX

Grammy

The enclosed letter had dropped onto Melinda's lap

when she opened the card. Along with it wafted the scent of Grammy. Baby powder and roses.

Grammy's hand cream of choice was always rose-scented.

Melinda couldn't help laughing through her tears. Grammy never lost her earthy sense of humor, even when the cancer limited her world to her bedroom those last few months. She shook her head and unfolded the lavender-colored paper.

Dear Melinda,

By now I've been gone at least a month. I told Jack to wait until the dust had settled, not just on my grave but in your lives.

Melinda honey, we've shared the best of our lives with each other. You and I have been blessed with a wonderful bond these past forty years. As much as I'd be the first to wish your father had been more available to you and that your mother had lived, it'd be a lie to say that I regret the consequences. It was a blessing to me, and to Jack, that we were able to spend so much time with you. Being able to raise you as our own for so much of your childhood meant everything to us.

We struggled financially while your dad was young and weren't able to spoil him the way we did you. But as you already know, spoiling you with material things wasn't ever our main focus. We wanted to spoil you with our love.

I've worried these last couple of years whether we've spoiled you too much. When things got rocky with you and Nicholas, I thought it might pass. All couples go through rough spots—that's just life. But then you picked up and moved to Washington, D.C., and your whole life revolved around Senator Hodge's career and agenda.

Jack and I were happy when you went to college right after high school and got your degree. We were so proud! And it always seemed destined that you'd marry Nicholas. Ever since you met him at St. Bonaventure, your eyes held a bright light.

We thought you were proud of his service in the Reserves and understood that it meant he could be called away at any time. So when he was called to war and you took it so badly, we questioned our assumptions. You said you believed that if Nicholas loved you, he wouldn't go. That he'd put family first.

Since you'd been unable to get pregnant I wondered if you worried he was leaving during the time you'd have left to get pregnant. Remember when I took you out for coffee and ordered you that huge maple scone? And you said, "I'm not supposed to eat refined sugar or wheat." I was trying to get you to relax, to enjoy yourself.

You've worried about so many things in your short life, Melinda.

It's clear to me that Nicholas is a true patriot and simply answered the call he always knew could come. Maybe he's even relished the challenge, in the way only a warrior does.

But you took it personally.

I'm sorry if this sounds like a lecture, Melinda. I just hate to see you suffer, and to see you throw away what may be the love of your life.

I know what pain that brings, as there was a time when I'd lost the love of my life. It was the bleakest period of my existence.

As you know, I've always liked writing. I'm sure you recall the column I wrote for the Buffalo Evening News. *But what you don't know is that my greatest work is what you're about to read. Mind you, I started it when I was young, idealistic and thought myself a cross between Jane Austen and James Joyce—unlikely though that sounds!*

I kept the journal hidden throughout the war but, just in case it was stolen or fell into the wrong hands, I wrote in English. Even though I was fluent, I was speaking my native French daily, so you may find some errors.

Read my story—you'll figure out quickly that it's not just my story but also that of Grandpa Jack, and millions of World War II survivors. Read this with an open mind and heart. Finally, understand why I found my peace and love here, in Buffalo.

Think about coming back to Buffalo, dearest, so you can give yourself a real life. I'll never believe that working in that rat race on Capital Hill is good for you, Melinda. You're certainly smart enough to be there with the best of them, but I don't want you to waste your heart on things that won't mean anything once you're my age. You were such a natural in the classroom. Your former students still ask about you.

I'm feeling bold, since you're not here in person to roll your beautiful blue eyes at me. I want you to reconsider your marriage to Nicholas. Twenty years of love and laughter—including the fifteen you've been married—is a lot to throw away, Melinda. Trust me when I tell you that no one will love you the way he has. I've seen both sides of love and marriage, and what you and Nicholas share is real.

I want to write more, but I've given you enough to read in my journals. I'd say "read it and weep" but unfortunately, I know you probably will. It is my prayer that you'll also find some things humorous, and that you may even find a reason to believe in love again.

XOX
Grammy

Melinda let the letter fall back onto her lap. Leave it to Grammy to think she could fix everyone's problems, even from the grave.

But her problems with Nicholas were about more than not having a baby. Their communication had broken down when she felt restless as a high-school English teacher. She'd wanted more.

"Why don't you write the great American novel?" Nick wanted to solve her problems for her.

"I'm not a novelist. I'm interested in politics, Nick. I really think I'm supposed to use my talents in this direction."

"Honey, I'm not being patronizing. But don't you think your restlessness is mostly due to your biological clock ticking away?"

Melinda had rejected his observation that this was all about her hormones. Sure, they'd been trying to conceive and nothing had happened, but it wasn't the entire focus of her life.

Or was it?

Nick had made his decision without her. He'd chosen to take another tour in Afghanistan. And she'd decided to take the job in D.C. without his help. They'd stopped relying on each other's judgment years ago.

All they had in common now was this house.

A house neither of them lived in anymore.

She plucked at the multicolored yarn on the afghan she'd snuggled into on the brown leather couch. Grammy meant well. She was a woman who'd always been with the love of her life, so Melinda understood the basis for Grammy's opinions.

But Grammy didn't understand that the situation

today wasn't the same as during World War II. Nick had a choice—whether or not to serve. Whether or not to break Melinda's heart.

Esmée's Journal

May 25, 1940

How can this be happening? How can men of intelligence bring us to our knees again? Haven't we suffered enough?

I've spent my entire academic life studying the Great War and how it destroyed our beloved Belgium. My family's strength, faith and resourceful nature are the only reasons I am able to write this entry today.

A scant generation later we've begun another ugly battle.

Ugly it is. The Germans have no room for anyone except themselves. They tolerate us, they use us. Over the past three weeks I've seen everything I've ever read about in my literature studies—and more.

Bloodthirsty warplanes bombed our capital, and smaller, tactical aircraft strafed my village's cow pastures. Douglas DuPont, who owns the fields behind our street, was shot dead while he tended to a birthing cow. His widow and five children are heartbroken and see no justification for his death.

Only Nazi barbarism.

My parents are quite vocal about what we're experiencing. They warn my sister and me of many years of sacrifice to come. Surely this won't last as long as the Great War. The Allies are on the right side of morality, of justice.

I will keep this record, so the world will know what happened. I will write in English—for practice and security.

Selfishly I wonder if I'll be able to continue my studies. I graduate in three weeks and plan to attend university this September.

The current situation may dictate otherwise. The simple act of taking the train into Brussels each day may well be impossible.

Does this mean life as I know it is extinguished?

July 15, 1940

Any hope of escape, of fleeing, is over now. I desperately wanted to run to the French border but Mother forbade it. Besides, with Elodie, who will take care of them? Elodie still can't walk without a lot of help, even using her cane. The polio could have been worse. Maman says I could have contracted it as well. But none of us did.

Just poor Elodie. My sweet little sister.

She looks more like ten years old than sixteen.

Maman and Papa are fine right now, but from what I've heard, the war will bring us all up against tough times. We could starve, or get sick, or both. Grandmère and Grandpère told us so many horrible stories of the Great War. I thought it was something I'd never experience. Yet here we are.

Maman and Papa need me, but I feel sorrowful over the loss of my hope, my plan, to study English literature. I can keep reading, of course, but how will I find books? The Nazis are already censoring newspapers and even library books. There are rumors the schools may close, as they did during the Great War.

If I am destined to remain in Belgium for the duration, I vow to make a difference. Not just to Maman, Papa and Elodie. But to my countrymen. To the boys from my class who've been forced to work in German factories. To the boys who've escaped to fight with our allies.

I wish I were a boy so I could carry a weapon, too.

I will find out what I can do.

Melinda knew Grammy studied English as a girl and spoke and wrote it fluently by the age of sixteen. Her breath caught as she realized that Esmée had kept such a detailed account of her life in a foreign tongue.

Esmée had high aspirations for a girl back then.

Esmée's Journal

September 14, 1940

My first wish has been granted. I'm officially a member of the Belgian Resistance! Maman and Papa are, too, but we associate with different groups. They're working with the older folks, doing more in the way of disrupting our occupiers' everyday misdeeds, like not cooperating when asked for papers or goods the Germans have no right asking for. But they have to be careful; if they anger the enemy and end up in jail, or worse, it won't help any of us.

I'm in a more active group. Right now, we're getting the local boys who stayed here in touch with their counterparts in England. Thank God for the radio. Still, we have to monitor each and every broadcast so as to not miss one clue the Allies might send us.

May 29, 1941

It's only been a year, but it feels like ten. I worry for us all. Our food has been so limited. If this war lasts much longer, we may starve before we're liberated from these evil bastards.

It's my duty to provide for Maman, Papa and Elodie. We can't expect Elodie to roam about the countryside looking for food or fuel to keep our house warm. Maman and Papa remain healthy but the war is wearing on them, and I see it reflected in the deepening lines on their faces, the sharper angle of their bent spines.

I pray for an answer.

Melinda took a sip of the tea that had grown cold and looked out the front window, past the Belgian lace curtains Grammy had ordered for her. It wasn't dark yet, but hazy with the gray that comes before a late-autumn sunset.

Her surroundings, which she'd taken for granted only a few journal entries ago, seemed luxurious, even excessive. On her drive up from D.C. she'd actually complained to herself that her leather car seats weren't heated.

Grammy had life-or-death issues to face when she was two decades younger than Melinda was now.

Esmée's Journal

June 1, 1941

A miracle may have happened today.

I met a young man, recently widowed, who owns a farm a few kilometers south of here. It's a little more rural than I'm used to, but the small town is familiar to me, as some of my schoolmates have gone there to live out the war with extended family.

His name is Henri. We met in Brussels at the Grand Place when I escaped to the city center, trying to remember what it used to be like. I was searching for some fresh vegetables for us, brought in from the countryside.

Henri handed me an apple.

He said he travels to Brussels to sell his produce as it comes in.

He's lonely, I see it in his eyes. And he has food. Enough for all of us.

June 5, 1941

Henri took me bicycle-riding in his town today. We rode the train to the station, and walked to his home. I didn't tell Maman and Papa what I was doing. They thought I was out doing Resistance work.

I was, but even Henri doesn't know that. I told the leader of my group in Brussels that I may have an opportunity to move out to the country-side, to Le Tourn. He told me they'd be happy to have me working there, since that's where many of the RAF insertions take place.

They warned me not to tell my new friend about my work. Just in case…

I can serve my country and keep my family fed with one simple vow.

June 10, 1941

Henri came by to meet my family today.

Maman and Papa were social enough, but I

could tell this is not a man they'd ever trust. Nothing concrete, just an undercurrent of distrust. When he left, they fired their questions at me.

"How did you meet him? How do you know he didn't find out you're Resistance and isn't going to turn you in? How can you be sure he's loyal to Belgium?"

I can't answer any of their questions without hesitation. But I know one thing—we won't starve if I marry him.

He is kind and polite to me. He's very interested in me, and although I'd normally not give his type a second glance, I have to be practical. I've never yet been in love, and with the war, I may never be. So why wait when I can marry a man who can provide for my family?

Henri? Grandpa's name was Jack. Had she been married before? Had this other man been her first husband?

Intrigued, Melinda turned the page to Grammy's next entry. She kept reading through 1941 and the start of 1942. Grammy married this Henri. The entries were bland at best, certainly no mention of undying love or passion. But nothing shocking, either.

Until she came upon an entry she'd never have believed Esmée Du Bois had written.

Esmée's Journal

March 17, 1942

I hate him. As much as I'm relieved to write these words, I'm trembling that he'll find me doing this. Or worse, he'll find this journal and use it as another excuse to slam me up against the cellar wall.

He's smart. He never hits me upstairs, where someone might see. No, he waits until I'm doing the laundry over the cellar fire, when I'm tired from the work and can't fight back, as well. Then he comes up to me, a snake in farmer's clothes, and sooner or later his hand reaches out and inflicts yet more pain.

If not for Belle, the Belgian Shepherd dog who showed up on our stoop last year, I'd have not one confidante. Henri threatened to get rid of her at first, but since she's grown to ninety pounds he leaves her be. I make sure their paths don't cross often. He's incapable of compassion for any living creature.

I couldn't go out to the market or see my family in Brussels for three weeks after the last beating. Can't risk hurting them. If they see me they'll know, even if they don't see the bruises under my clothes. They'll see the despair in my eyes.

I thought I'd done well for my family by

marrying Henri. His kind words and thoughtful manner before our marriage seduced me, as did the food he'd provide for my family.

I never imagined what horrors awaited me.

Oh, Maman and Papa. Elodie! I miss them so much. They are also active in the Resistance and I fear for their capture. Yet they wouldn't be my family if they didn't do what they believed in.

And I've been able to keep them fed. Potatoes, beets, even some meat when Henri slaughters one of our remaining cattle. We have to stretch the meat, using a little at a time, but it keeps our bellies full enough. The hunger pains don't hurt or distract as they did before I married this bastard.

Although, there are days I'm too nauseated to eat from the ferocity of his attacks.

April 16, 1942

The one good thing that remains is my Resistance work. He has no idea about it and never will. At first I didn't tell him to protect him. Now I don't tell him for fear of being killed, and all my work being for naught.

The group needs me. They need my information, my language abilities. I don't speak fluent German but I understand enough to know when the bastards are planning another domestic raid.

My English has improved, too, since I've worked with the RAF intelligence planted here.

Originally I'd thought that when I married Henri, he might support me in providing a safe landing spot for the spies England sends us.

I will *never* tell him about my Resistance work. It's what sustains me, even more than protecting my family. When he's smashing my jaw or I crack another tooth on a door frame from his strike, I just think of what our young boys are going through. We will persevere.

Belgium will be free again, thanks to our strength of will and our Allied angels.

Like manna from heaven they float down, infiltrate our society and use the information they glean to help the analysts back in London.

The war will end quickly.

Our Allies are strong.

If only I felt as strong. This morning, as he does every morning, Henri wanted me upon wakening. I'd prefer to keep our relations in the dark. It's easier if I don't have to see the devil when I have to suffer the weight of him.

And the brutality of his lovemaking. It's not lovemaking; it's forced violence. He rapes me every time. Except I don't resist. What good would it do? He'd just knock me out with a blow and have at it anyhow. At least this way I can get up and do my best to wash away any chance of his seed implanting.

May 24, 1942

He's angry. It's almost a year and no whisper of a baby yet. At thirty-five he doesn't want to wait. While I, at almost 21, pray he'll die in his sleep, God forgive me.

I pray I can have babies with real love one day.

Even as I write this, I can't say I believe love exists anymore. Not when my Jewish friends are being murdered, not when I'm beaten senseless for not making my *pommes de terre* tender enough.

I made a horrible mistake last week. In a moment of weakness, when Henri again mentioned his anger at no child from me, I suggested we could adopt. I have contacts. I didn't tell him this, of course. With luck, we could adopt a Jewish baby. One whose parents have been sent away or will be soon. Several families in our town have adopted these babies, though it's done quietly, without fanfare.

We could save a life and might even have a chance at saving our marriage.

At changing his heart.

He answered by shoving my head into the tub of water I'd used to wash the dishes.

"Do you desire a slow miserable death?

That's what the Gestapo will give us both if they hear your filthy talk. The only babies in this house will be mine."

He kept ranting as he pulled on my hair, allowing me to gasp for air, then plunging my face back into the dirty water.

Sometimes I think of a different day, when I was young and looked forward to life and love. Before the Germans came back to our beautiful country and stamped out any hope of freedom.

Chapter 3

Esmée's Journal

November 23, 1942

Winter is upon us. But my heart is far colder than any wind from the North Sea.

Yesterday I saw the ultimate betrayal. More painful than any of his slaps or punches or kicks.

I watched that bastard, my husband, give food—first-quality harvest and three pigs—to our enemy. He smiled and laughed, and even smoked a cigarette with them. He doesn't think I saw them. He thinks I was busy in the cellar, boiling our linens. I fumed inside as he sold his soul for our country's blood.

Thank you, God, that I never told him about my involvement in the Resistance.

Now I'll have to be more careful than ever when I go out, which can only be when he's either passed out from beer or when he goes into Brussels, which is rarer. I used to think he went into Brussels just to sell his goods, but now I wonder if he's been making friends with the Germans all along. Maybe he's charming one of their vile wives?

No matter to me. I am determined to get my family, my real family, through the war. I pray his seed never takes root inside me. God forgive me, I don't want a child with this devil.

Melinda closed Grammy's book and leaned her head against the back of the worn leather reading chair. She needed a break. It was as if the venom in Grammy's words could burn Melinda's skin more than sixty years after they were written.

She shoved her feet into her scuffed slippers and went to the kitchen to make a large pot of tea. She looked at the antique clock on the wall; she'd wound it last night.

She and Nicholas had bought this clock together, during a visit to Niagara-on-the-Lake. The intricate carving on the simple wooden box was yet another reminder of her own love gone bad.

Here it was, eight-thirty on a Saturday evening.

Dinner wasn't even an option. Her stomach was as tense as her nerves. Tea was the only thing that ever helped her through these times, and there'd been many cups in the last few years.

The backyard light flicked on, evident through the toile curtains that hung halfway down the picture window, which ran the length of the kitchen.

Despite her nervousness, Melinda walked over to the door. Probably just some wayward raccoon or neighborhood cat, but it never hurt to check. She'd been living in the heart of D.C. for too long to ignore any hint of danger.

The baseball bat she kept at her bedside was upstairs. Her fingers itched for it. As she stood in the middle of the kitchen floor, the teapot started to whistle.

The figure of a large man loomed in the window of the kitchen door. Melinda screamed.

And then her brain registered what her eyes saw.

"Nicholas!" His name was a strange mix of strangled cry and whispered prayer. Before her feet could respond to her brain's order to move, Nicholas had unlocked the door and it swung open.

He looked as tall and imposing as ever, albeit a bit slimmer than she remembered. He was bundled against the cold in a charcoal overcoat.

He'd always been the most attractive man she'd known, and still was. Her gaze went to his face, and met his blue eyes that, right now, blazed fire at her.

He hadn't expected her any more than she had him.

"What are you—"

"Why are you screaming at me?"

They both spoke at once. Their eye contact remained steady while the words hung in the frosty air between them.

"It's freezing in here." She broke the contact and nodded at the door he'd left wide-open behind him.

"Don't want that, do we?" He slammed the door shut with his foot, never moving his eyes from her face.

But the motion of his foot distracted her, and she glanced down.

And saw the cane.

She tried to look away before he saw her discovery but wasn't quick enough.

His eyes narrowed, his mouth curled. He'd never accepted pity from anyone.

"You're hurt?" Her words came out in a squeak.

"Nothing major." He tapped the cane on the tile. "This helps me negotiate uneven ground—or with an intruder in my home."

"You don't have to be so snippy. It's still legally half *my* home—for the next two weeks."

She walked to the teakettle and took it from the hot stove. She hoped her actions conveyed a tranquility she didn't feel. First Grammy's venomous words and now Nicholas's censorious presence.

"'Snippy.' Yeah, that's how I'm feeling. Snippy."

He strode across the room to the coat closet, the cane tapping in rhythm with his steps. The rustle of hangers and winter coats was followed by a muffled curse, just loud enough to reach her ears.

She stopped plunging her teabag into the cup.

It wasn't like Nicholas to swear. At least it hadn't been, not while they were married. Or rather, together.

Melinda bit her lip. How could she know what he was like now? They hadn't communicated in more than six months. Not one e-mail, not one phone call.

There'd been times when Melinda itched to take advantage of her staff position in Senator Hodge's office and use a Pentagon resource to trace Nicholas's location.

But she hadn't.

If Nicholas wanted her, he could find her.

He'd been in Afghanistan, last she'd heard. He could've died and she wouldn't have known. Not until the casualty assistance officer knocked on her door. If Nicholas had even bothered to change her emergency-contact information after she'd left Buffalo.

"What are you doing here?"

"Aaagh!" Melinda dropped the bag she'd steeped too long in the hot water and whirled to face Nicholas.

Don't look at his eyes. Don't remember why you loved him.

"Shouldn't I be asking you that? In case you haven't checked, I've had no information from you in the past six months—except the divorce papers I was served with four months ago!"

She stared at him, as surprised by her outburst as he obviously was.

After a long moment, he glanced away. The anger that fueled her accusation ebbed but left her knees shaky. Melinda sank into the 1940s-style red-and-white striped chair nearest to her and looked down at the tiled floor.

Anywhere but at his eyes.

She heard the scrape of a chair, then a vibration as the table shook with Nicholas's weight against it.

"You never responded to the papers, except to sign them." His voice was flat. Melinda's tension flared into resentment at his apparent nonchalance.

"What was I supposed to do, Nicholas? The last thing I knew, we were separating to see if living apart was what we actually wanted. I didn't realize you'd already made up your mind."

She hated sounding so pathetic but there it was. The truth as she saw it.

"The last thing *I* knew, you packed up and left for D.C.—a week before I had to ship out." His quiet tone tugged at her and she risked another look at him.

She gazed openly at his strong features and noted that his skin appeared paler, more drawn. The lines that crinkled when he laughed made him look tired, even sad. But his eyes bore the intensity she'd always seen in him and for a second Melinda didn't know how she'd lived without her husband these past months.

"What else could I do? I was reacting to the news

that you were leaving again the best way I knew how." Her words ended on a whisper, and she looked down at her hands.

Her bare hands. She wore her wedding ring on a thick gold chain around her neck. It had been Grammy's chain from before World War II. Had he noticed?

His sigh reverberated around her. "Doesn't matter now, Melinda. We've made our choices." His fingers drummed on the table and she saw that he, too, had removed his wedding band. She didn't think it was for safety purposes since he wasn't in uniform.

"How long will you be here?" His question caught her off guard. She had Senator Hodge's blessing to take at least two weeks.

"I don't know." Maybe Nicholas needed some time alone here, she thought, before they put the house on the market. Their home.

"Do you need me to be out of here?" she asked.

"This is your home, too, Melinda. All I want to know is whether I'm sleeping on the couch for tonight or if I should go ahead and unpack in the guest room."

"Grandpa Jack gave me this journal of Grammy's to read, and his diary. I'd planned to stay with him—do whatever he might need me to do before winter sets in. But he insisted I stay here."

She shrugged, trying to appear casual. "I think it would've upset him too much if I fought him on this."

Nicholas's expression remained impassive. "Fine.

Take your time," he said. "I'm home for good, so after about a week or so I'll be back at work full-time."

His stamina was close to his pre-injury level. But he hadn't had to test it in a real environment for so long.

His leg ached from the flight and the drive home. But he was secure in the knowledge that no one—not Melinda or anyone else—could tell just how much his active-duty stint in Afghanistan had cost him.

Esmée's Journal

December 19, 1942

My hands shake as I write. This has to be the coldest winter on record. Or do I feel the damp penetrating every inch of my body because fear has left me hollow?

I managed to bring Maman and Papa enough turnips and potatoes to get them through the next week or so. I hid them in the folds of my old wool coat, which grows thinner each day.

I caught Henri snooping about our room and pawing through my few possessions. Having to act as if that didn't bother me wasn't difficult, as this journal, this account of my hell, is the only thing of value to me in the house.

I keep it hidden behind the old tapestry that hangs in our sitting area. The entire wall appears to be plain old brick. Several of them are loose, but I've dug out a hole behind one brick. I then placed another brick in the hole to the right, so that anyone who pulls out the front brick and reaches in will find an empty space.

I live in fear that he'll learn about my work with the Resistance. Yet death would be preferable to the humiliation he brings with his ugliness and dark heart. There are times I want to take my rolling pin and crush his skull with it. But where would I go? To prison? Then my family would starve.

I will hang on as long as I can. As long as there's food for Maman, Papa and Elodie.

The stove fights me each day. Henri has a stash of wood he monitors closely. If I use too much he smacks me. If I allow the fire to burn out, he uses his belt.

I live for the times he travels to Brussels, or wherever he goes. The house isn't peaceful unless he's out of it.

I told Philippe in our group that I live on a farm, and if I know that Henri will be gone long enough, our Allies could use one of our fields as a safe place for RAF insertions.

December 21, 1942

The phone rang the other day and I answered, hoping for news from Maman and Papa. Henri was out in the field, earlier than usual. I picked up the receiver and before I could say "Hallo," I heard a string of German before the caller hung up.

For some reason—pure luck?—we're one of the few homes that still has our phone line connected.

So now they call Henri at home. What kind of creature is he that he supports the enemy so blatantly during our worst years in Belgium? While my male classmates and cousins fight God-knows-where for our release and freedom from these bastards.

I long for the day the Germans will go home. If it's up to me, they'll go home in shame, having lost to our Allies.

And Henri will go with them. If I live that long, I'll divorce him as soon as the War is over. I don't care if it ruins my life. He already has. Divorce will ruin my reputation but will save my soul. What's left of it.

Chapter 4

Esmée's Journal

December 25, 1942

This is a Christmas I will always remember.

I now have a man to nurse back to health and a husband to grieve. I don't grieve for Henri, but I grieve for the marriage that never was. For the hope I had at the beginning. For the hope of what I once thought was a mutual friendship that might blossom into a true marriage.

Let me start again.

I've learned during the past weeks that Henri has helped the Germans rout out the Jewish children from our village. He even knew where they were staying if they'd been sent to relatives.

As he beat me for what would be the last time, he snarled, "I'll bet you think they're the same as us, don't you? Don't you?" I said nothing. I couldn't; my lip was swollen and bleeding. But I laughed inside as I knew that once I told the Group what Henri was up to, they'd take care of him. And I *had* to tell them. It wasn't about my conscience or my soul. It was about saving innocent lives. The Nazis occupy our country but they can't take my heart. And I'd die before my husband (in name only) could give them one more piece of information.

I went to Midnight Mass on my own on Christmas Eve. I figured Henri had some urgent evil business, so I went to pray it wouldn't work out well.

The night was cold and crisp. For once we had no rain, just a wide clear sky above, with the stars floating close enough to touch. I relished my walk home in the dark. This isn't a Christmas for parties and celebration; it's one for prayer and hope that our hell will end soon.

I came home from Mass to an empty house. But Henri wasn't passed out drunk on the sofa, as usual, nor was he waiting to pummel me. A frigid breeze blew through the house and I heard my dog, Belle, barking out back. Henri was always careful to make sure she was outside when he beat me—Belle would have killed him if he'd ever left her in the same room when he hurt me.

Her barks alarmed me with their persistence. I ran through the house to the kitchen door, which stood wide open. I could see a lantern about halfway across the field, which was lit up by the full, full moon. I made out Henri's silhouette and Belle's, across from him. But who was the figure next to Belle?

I grabbed one of Henri's hunting rifles. I may never know why I did; I'd never allowed Henri to find out that I knew how to fire a weapon. He would've locked up the rifles, and for some perverse reason I've always felt safe knowing they were there. Just in case.

I ran into the field, the frozen mud crunching so loudly beneath my feet that the sound drowned out whatever Henri was saying to Belle, and to the figure. As I neared, I realized with a jolt that Henri wasn't even aware of my approach. Belle's barks had helped to cover my steps, but that's not why he was distracted.

Henri was enraged. But for once, not at me.

"You stupid shit of the earth. Do you think I don't know who you are, what you represent?" Henri had his rifle up and cocked, pointed at the figure.

It was a man. He wore plain dark clothes and

there was a large cloth draped on the ground next to him.

A parachute.

The Group had said they'd use my pasture, but they'd give me advance notice—if they could. Obviously they hadn't.

"Please, friend, let me explain." The man spoke perfect Belgian French. Henri started to yell at him in German.

"I'm not your friend, nor am I a friend of any supporter of Churchill's."

"I don't understand," the man answered, again in fluent French, but I had the sense that he understood Henri perfectly. At this point he'd spotted me, although I noticed he gave away nothing in his expression. He was sitting, both legs in front of him. He held his right ankle in his hands.

"Understand *this*. You'll be sorry you didn't break your neck in the fall." Henri raised his barrel and from his stance I knew he was a stroke from killing the man.

"Henri, don't!"

Henri barely started. He didn't even look at me.

"Shut up, Esmée. Take Belle back in the house before I shoot her, too. You know not to disobey me."

Disobey him?

I hoisted my rifle and shot Henri in the head.

His body dropped in slow motion, and I wish

I could tell you I felt guilt or recrimination or
compassion at his fate. But all I felt is what I feel
now. If I must suffer in hell for Henri's blood,
better that than letting him spill the blood of more
innocent Jewish families. God only knows how
many have met their untimely fate at his hands,
through his help.

"Nice shot."

Again, the stranger spoke in fluent French and
I responded the same way.

"I just saved your ass and all you say is 'nice
shot'?"

"Merry Christmas?" he offered, and I laughed.

I actually *laughed*. I, who had just murdered
my husband in cold blood, after Christmas Mass.
War does strange things to a person, and sadly I'm
no exception.

After our laughter stopped, we were left with
the still, cold night and the prospect of figuring
out if indeed this man belonged here. And what
was I to do with him?

I studied him more closely. He looked like any
local Belgian. A full beard and spectacles covered
most of his face. I couldn't see much more in the
dark, no matter how bright the moon. But he had
a quiet, intense presence about him.

"You are Muriel."

He spoke my Resistance code name. He'd
heard Henri call me "Esmée." Still, he could be

an undercover German. A double agent. But at that moment I decided to trust him.

"Yes, I am."

"I am from across the way."

This time he spoke in English.

He meant, of course, the English Channel. He was another one of the many Allied operatives who were landing in Belgium to help the Resistance.

I put down my rifle. It ran through my mind that this Ally probably thought I was crazy. That I could stand there having a calm chat with him in my cow pasture on Christmas morning, as my husband's body lay next to us.

"Did you love him?" His question shocked me. I responded before I could think.

"I hated him."

"So saving my ass wasn't too much of a sacrifice, then?"

"No."

I wish I'd been able to explain to him that I wasn't a monster. That years of living with this horrible man in a horrible time had left me with no hope for my future. That my only reason for getting up each morning has been to save more people from the Germans, and to save any future victims of Henri's efforts to aid the enemy.

But all I said was "no."

Melinda heaved the journal off her lap and placed it on the mahogany end table she and Nicholas had refinished last year.

The conversation they'd had then played in her mind as if it had just happened.

She'd landed a position in Senator Hodge's local office but she'd been offered one in Washington, D.C. She'd wanted to take it. *Planned* to take it.

Nicholas had rejected her suggestion that they move. His accounting practice was flourishing and, even though he'd have no problem landing a great job in D.C., he didn't want to leave western New York.

"It's all we've ever known. We've been so happy here," he'd argued.

"Exactly. It's all we've ever known. But it was pretty damned desolate while you were in Afghanistan."

She'd loathed the entire year he'd been gone, and was grateful he'd returned in one piece.

But the year of separation and isolation had stirred a restlessness in Melinda that she needed to explore. She was like her father, James, who'd worked as a civil servant, first for the municipal government in Buffalo and then in Arizona. She was interested in federal politics. Grammy, like Nick, had thought maybe it was time they had a baby, but the baby never came.

They'd been unable to conceive.

"Honey, we're in an adjustment period," he'd said that fall day. "I've only been back six months, and we were apart an entire year." He'd placed his hands on her shoulders, but Melinda couldn't accept any comfort from him. Not then.

"You've only been home for six months but you're already talking about leaving again." Her words were spoken quietly but their weight was deadly.

Nicholas dropped his hands from her shoulders and took a step backward.

"You've always supported my Reserve training before. Surely you understood it was training for war."

"Yes, but you seem so eager to go, Nick. It's as though you have some sort of death wish. I mean, to agree, *to volunteer* again—"

"Cut me some slack here, Melinda. I've been with the same team for the past ten years. We're like family. I can't let them down now."

"What about me? Us?"

"There's always us. That never changes."

"You say you want a baby, but how can we work on it when you're halfway around the world fighting in a war?"

"The same way we'll work on it while you're in D.C. and I'm here." His resentment at her more and more frequent business trips was reflected in his tone.

They'd thrown accusations at each other that day as if words didn't hurt, wouldn't stay ingrained on their hearts for a long while to come, if not forever.

On Sunday morning, Nicholas rose with the sun. Mornings were always the toughest time. He had to stretch, put on his prosthesis and remember how to walk with his new leg. Sometimes the phantom pain took his breath away. Not today.

Today he was under the same roof as Melinda. His heartache far outweighed any pain he'd suffered as a result of the IED, improvised explosive device, and the subsequent loss of his leg.

The pain he felt at the loss of his squad mate, Tommy, who hadn't survived the IED, could still leave him breathless if he dwelled on it. But it didn't compare to the pain he felt at the thought of losing Melinda.

Waking up in the trauma unit and finding out that Tommy had died, leaving a widow and three kids, was a gut-wrenching blow. He wasn't sure if he'd ever get over it. He'd certainly never forget Tommy.

But if he lost Melinda, their marriage, he'd lose his most important reason to live.

Melinda was his life, his soul mate. But they'd gone wrong somewhere in their fifteen-year marriage. He intended to right whatever he'd screwed up.

He went downstairs and started a pot of coffee. He was happy to see that Melinda had replaced the Starbucks coffee he'd left in the cupboard seven months ago. While the coffee brewed, he walked to the front door, intent on the morning paper. After he opened the front door and was greeted with an icy blast he realized the paper service had been terminated.

Of course. He'd made the call himself two days before his departure.

A week after Melinda had left.

"You're up early." Her voice seemed to touch the tender place inside that he'd thought was dead.

"Habit." He turned away from her, and went back into the kitchen. But not before he caught a whiff of her morning scent. Shampoo, hair products, perfume. For a split second, all their bitter words dissolved and all he wanted was to pull her into his arms.

Instead, he settled for looking at her.

Big mistake. The IED had taken his leg but, thank God, nothing else. Right now he was acutely aware of his physiological response to her.

Big blue eyes stared at him from behind fringed lashes that he knew to be pale blond when not coated with mascara, as they were now. She'd cut her hair, and as much as he missed the straight, silky length that fell to her shoulders, the new sleek chin-length style was stunning on her.

When she raised an eyebrow, Nicholas turned away. He had to stay cool if he was going to pull this one off.

"Learn anything interesting from Grammy's journal?" He poured them each a cup of coffee. He was generous with her half-and-half, just the way she liked it.

Melinda's expression looked as if she'd refuse his attempt at a truce. After a few tense moments, the lines in her face relaxed.

He watched her slim hands wrap around the ceramic mug. She lifted it to her lips and he had to avert his gaze or risk another surge of hormones.

"I've—" she narrowed her eyes "—*we've* always

known that Grammy was a strong person. But I'm reading about someone I don't know at all."

She related what she'd read so far, and while Nick was saddened that Grammy had suffered at the hands of an abusive husband, he wasn't surprised to learn how resourceful she'd been.

"This guy who landed in her pasture—he was a Brit, I assume? Grandpa Jack?"

Nick took a long sip of coffee and watched her across the kitchen table. The sun was rising and sent slanted beams of light across Melinda's face.

"I haven't read that far yet. They always said they met during the war, didn't they?"

"Yes, but neither one of them ever told me the full story. They were experts at enjoying today, the here and now."

Nicholas longed to share the last conversation he'd had with Grammy. But not now. Not until Melinda was ready to hear him out. After he'd told her about his leg.

Melinda sighed.

"It's weird. I thought I was coming home to take care of Grandpa Jack. You know how lifetime couples often pass on very close to each other? I've been expecting to hear Grandpa's gone, too. Instead, I come home to find him in his garden, working away, and he gives me these journals to read. Tells me they're very important."

She swished her coffee around in her mug.

"I keep thinking I should feel more grief or an extra closeness to Grammy as I read this. But like I said, it's as though I'm reading the story of another woman's life."

She stood up and went to the refrigerator.

"Most of us don't see our parents or grandparents in an objective light, the way the world sees them."

Nick smiled to himself as Melinda pulled out eggs, cheese, vegetables and Tabasco sauce. She was making them an omelet. Did she realize how easily they'd slipped back into their Sunday-morning breakfast routine?

Minus the lovemaking, of course.

"True. But, Nick, she killed a man!"

Melinda's voice snapped him back.

"I see what you mean." He shook his head. "Hell, she wouldn't even let me kill the slugs that were eating her prize tomatoes two summers ago. She said 'just let me take them down to the creek.'"

"Right, exactly." She cracked two more eggs against the ceramic mixing bowl.

He studied Mel's movements about the counter and stove. God, he'd missed her grace, her warmth.

"You know, Mel, We're all capable of things we wouldn't have any reason to think about unless—or until—we're faced with the circumstances."

What would Melinda think of him if she knew he'd killed? Even in self-defense, in war.

What if she knew about the hatred he'd carried in his heart for the person or persons who were responsible for the IED that killed his friend and blew his leg off?

Chapter 5

"Have you ever had to kill anyone, Nick?"

Her question sucked the air from his lungs. She'd never asked about his time in Afghanistan. After his first return, she'd spoken only of the future, mostly about her desired transfer to D.C.

This new intimacy wasn't much, but he'd take it.

"I've been in a war, Melinda. What do you think?"

He saw her shoulders tense. She stopped whisking the eggs and turned to look at him.

"I suppose you've had to do things I don't want to know about."

"You're correct."

Melinda turned back to the counter. A few minutes

later, she sat down with two full plates of omelet, sliced melon and rye toast. Drool threatened to drip from the sides of Nick's mouth as he stared at their meal.

"This is incredible, Mel." He hadn't had a home-made meal in, what, seven, eight months?

She dug her fork into the fluffy omelet and raised it to her lips. Only then did she meet his gaze, and laughed.

"You act like you haven't eaten in years, Nick."

"It was a long trip home." He couldn't say any more or he'd scare her with his newfound devotion to their marriage.

So he shoved a forkful of egg into his mouth.

This was going to be far more difficult than he'd imagined. He didn't want to overwhelm her with his emotions. Their marriage had broken down over a long time. He didn't expect to mend it in one conversation.

"Let me warm up our coffee."

She went to the counter and he was grateful for the reprieve. There was so much at stake here. Because if he didn't win Melinda back before the divorce was final, he'd lose the biggest part of himself.

The best part.

"I'd appreciate it, thanks." He needed to switch gears or his emotions were going to become obvious.

"Have you heard from David?" Melinda's half brother still lived in Buffalo but rarely came around. He was always too busy with the next deal in local real estate.

"Not since the funeral." She sipped her coffee. "He

isn't as close to Grandpa as I am. Besides, he and Tari spend a lot of time with the kids."

Kids we never had.

Nick sighed.

"Just because they're raising children doesn't mean you can't ask for some help if you need it with Jack."

Melinda's face was relaxed, her expression thoughtful. This was how it was supposed to be between them. How it *had* been, before they'd both screwed things up.

"I'm not afraid to ask him, if that's what you're getting at. But I don't see any need to bother him at this point. Grandpa's doing fine from what I saw yesterday. He's even cooking for himself."

"Did the casseroles from the neighbors run out?"

Melinda laughed.

"The original round, yes, but several of the widows keep bringing him a fresh meal every few days or so."

"No one's asked to marry him yet?" Nick smiled at her. There'd never been anyone but Esmée for Jack. And the widows knew it, too. Still, they couldn't resist feeding the neighborhood's most eligible senior.

"I hope not. That's the last thing he needs."

"Still, it has to be a welcome distraction from his grief."

Melinda looked at him, her eyes large.

"When did you get so introspective?"

"Every now and then I actually do reveal some human characteristics, Mel."

Esmée's Journal

February 1, 1943

The man with the broken ankle will only tell me his name is "Mac." But I doubt that's his real name. I went through all his clothes as I washed them but there's no identification, no indication of who he is or where he came from.

I'm almost positive he's RAF, or an agent for the Brits. No matter, as we're all on the same side. We speak in a mixture of French and English.

Philippe from the Resistance Group has become invaluable to me. He and three other members came and took care of Henri's body. Philippe told me to tell my neighbors, family and friends that Henri went away on Christmas Eve and never came back. He wouldn't be the first Belgian to disappear in the middle of the night. No one questioned my explanation.

I live in fear of a German soldier rapping on my door, demanding to know what I've done with Henri, but so far it hasn't happened.

I should worry more about how I'll explain my new visitor. Yet none of my neighbors even know of him. Since I helped him into the house that night only a little over a month ago, he's remained hidden from them.

I've been able to keep Maman and Papa away

thanks to the cold weather. I don't want them im-
plicated in any of my doings.

February 3, 1943

I've seen him looking at me. At first his
glances were questioning, as though he was trying to figure out how I could have shot my husband. He speaks to Philippe in quiet, hushed tones
whenever he stops over. Philippe tells me nothing
except "You're doing a great patriotic service to
your country, Esmée."

When I joined the Resistance I understood that
I'd be given many tasks I would not be able to ask
the *why* or *how* of. That lack of information is to
protect our cause, ourselves and our Allies. Even
if we're captured and tortured, we can't give the
enemy what we don't know.

But I long to find out more about Mac. Where
is he from? What lies behind those dark blue eyes
that watch me with such intense interest through
the coldest months of the year?

His eyes reveal more to me than he realizes.
When he first arrived, during those terrible days
after Henri died, his eyes would glaze over with
pain, or from fever, and show me his need. Need
for healing, for comfort, yes, but I saw more in
his eyes. I saw his soul.

This is a good man, perhaps haunted by something, some need I can't identify.

I haven't craved a man's touch in so long. When my marriage to Henri went sour early on, I sometimes fantasized about having a husband who really loved me, whose caresses I cherished. But as my reality became more and more gruesome, it wasn't worth the pain to tease myself with fantasies of a happy relationship.

The longer Henri is gone, the more aware I become of my own needs. I'm twenty-one years old. I'm no longer a girl. I know what goes on in the marriage bed, physically if not emotionally and spiritually. I can imagine how a true joining would be.

But to imagine it with Mac—have I lost my mind? Perhaps one of Henri's slaps or punches wiped out my sanity and common sense.

A man's touch, other than my father's, has only brought me suffering.

Yet my fingers itch to touch Mac.

I did touch him, when I cleansed him, and when he had the fever. I told myself it was to soothe him, but even in his sweat-drenched sleep I wanted to touch him. To feel that the skin over his bones was real. That *he* was real. That my nightmare with Henri had ended.

I protected his privacy, of course. I helped him

with the bedpan as much as he needed, but kept my eyes averted.

All right, I did get a glance. Or two.

Mac is an attractive man.

Or would I find any man who isn't beating me attractive?

February 4, 1943

Mac's socks are taking longer than I expected. I keep dropping stitches when he speaks, which has been more often lately. I speak to him of my hopes for the future, always careful to leave it simple. To let him think that I have my own life to get back to after the war.

He is so endearing, even when the pain or his restlessness makes him cranky.

I had to put my pen down a minute—I thought I heard Mac's bell tinkling from his room. But he's still sound asleep. It's twelve-thirty in the morning and I can't sleep. I should be exhausted these days. The simple act of bathing myself, of using the bathroom, is a strain in the cold. We have an indoor toilet, but it's off the kitchen and not heated. I dread removing even one layer of clothing, let alone stripping down to wash. Each day I have to make sure my windows are blackened so the house won't draw the attention of the Germans.

There's only one explanation for my desire to remain awake, to savor every minute of every day.

Mac.

His steps are stronger and his complexion looks healthy now. Even on the meager potatoes and scraps of pork I manage, he's healed.

I can't think about his departure. It's crazy, I know. When this man dropped into my life, I was already deciding to leave Henri. Instead, I killed him.

Yet Mac seems to like me. He's never judged me for my sin.

Whenever I see Mac, I can't help feeling all warm inside. His presence makes me aware of my body as I've never been before. My hands tremble, my skin tingles, and I swear, I can feel my blood's heat as it courses across my breasts and down my stomach… No one's ever made me feel such things before.

This must be one of those wartime events that Maman and Papa talk about. What else can explain it?

February 5, 1943

Mac will be gone soon. I can tell. He's bearing more weight on his ankle and he no longer sweats from the pain.

I will miss our conversations. Today he made

me laugh at least half a dozen times as I tried to complete my kitchen chores.

"Why do you clean the floor when it will just get dirty again? Wouldn't you rather sit here and be bowled over by my charm?"

Just then I bowled over the bucket of water I'd been using and created a flood in front of the sink. The same sink Henri had smashed my head against, yet here I was with Mac, laughing.

If it weren't for my family's near-starvation I'd think I was living in a dream. But this isn't a dream. It's my life, and my life has collided with history. This war is like no other, mostly—I'm ashamed to admit—because it's happened to me.

February 10, 1943

Mac has gotten so much better this past week. The fever's finally gone.

When I'm with Mac I forget my burdens, the fact that I had to murder my husband not just to save Mac's life but my own soul. I focus on making Mac comfortable. From what Philippe has told me, Mac is an integral part of the Belgian Resistance plans. He's English but speaks flawless French, Flemish and German. So he's a linguist. A linguist who parachuted onto my pasture.

Not by accident.

I don't ask him about his work; it would be wrong if he told me. Besides, he won't. Just knowing he's one of us is good enough for me.

Our conversations aren't easily described, so the best I can do is try to record them here.

"Esmée, what are you knitting today?" he asked the other day. Belle lay at my feet, where she's taken up permanent residence now that Henri's gone.

"Socks."

"For your parents?"

"No."

I didn't want to admit that I'd started a pair for him. It seemed too personal—what my hands touched would be worn against his body.

"Then for whom?"

"For a friend."

"You don't have any friends who come and visit. It's someone from before the war, then?"

"There is no one from before the war. Once I made the mistake of marrying Henri—" my voice caught and I hated the betrayal of my self-loathing "—I lost my friends. Henri didn't want me out of the house more than necessary."

I knit the next row of stitches on the old wooden needles.

"At first I thought he was being protective of me because of the war. I never would've married him if I'd known how he was. But I was duped."

"You're too smart to have been duped."

"You'd think so, but no, my common sense when it comes to men is no larger than a pea."

"You berate yourself too much."

His words were quiet and sincere. I wasn't prepared for the tears that fell from my lowered eyes. Plop, plop, onto the worn old wool. I wiped up the unwanted mess.

"He did that to me."

"Esmée—"

Out of the corner of my eye, I saw him reach toward me. Instinctively I flinched and ducked away, even though he was more than four feet from me, lying on the bed. He couldn't have touched me without significant effort on his part. Still, I'd reacted as though he was going to strike me.

"What did he do to you, Esmée?"

"What any man of his disposition does. He treated me like he'd treat a dog."

I sniffled and started knitting again.

"But what he didn't figure on is that I'm smarter than a dog." I smiled briefly. "Even a dog like my darling Belle." I grew serious again. "I knew what he was doing when he went into Brussels and when he sold our goods to the enemy."

"How did you keep your Resistance work from him?"

"I told him I was going to my parents', or to buy wool from the woman at the other end of town."

"What woman?"

"Fabienne Peroux. She is part of our efforts, but also has an impressive stash of wool that she's reclaimed from old sweaters, socks and the like. I've been able to make sweaters for every member of the family since the war started."

"Always thinking of others, aren't you, Esmée?"

"Please. Don't think of putting me on any pedestal. I'm just doing what any other Belgian is doing during a difficult time. And look around— I have a roof over my head, clothes on my back. I can bathe when I need to, and I haven't gone hungry yet. Neither have Maman, Papa or Elodie."

"I understand, Esmée. I have a family back home, too, you know. I understand what it's like to take care of everyone else at your own expense. Sometimes it's virtuous, sometimes it's just habit. But every now and then we need to ask ourselves if it's for other motives."

"Such as?"

"Such as needing to keep so busy we don't have time to think of our own needs."

I allowed his words to sink in for a row of purl stitches.

"It certainly helps the days pass more quickly."

Mac laughed.

"Of course it does. But what if you were to die tomorrow? Have you done all you want to in your lifetime, Esmée?"

"Why do you insist on asking such serious questions?"

I had one of my own. Was Mac married?

"By the way, my family is my mother and father and sisters. I've never been married."

He'd read my mind.

I had to hide my joy, my relief.

Daylight streaked through the window, the shade open for its usual few hours.

"Look, for once the sun is shining in Belgium. You're on the mend, and will be able to aid our efforts soon. I'm free of the chains that bound me these past two years."

"But are you free of *your* chains, Esmée?"

Heat suffused my chest and inched up my neck and onto my cheeks.

"We're never sure about tomorrow, Mac. Why worry about all this nonsense now?"

"Because we may not have tomorrow to make things right."

He paused and his scrutiny left me breathless. Honestly, I feel like such a wanton around him. How can he not see my attraction to him?

"So tell me, Esmée, since you didn't answer

my question in the first place. What more do you want out of life?"

I answered him. "I don't want to ever worry again about what I do in my own home. I want to have babies and raise them to be joyous, happy and free. I want to teach my daughter to knit and cook, and my son to grow up in a free world, where he'll never worry about going to war."

"Sounds to me like you'd be willing to get married again. To trust again."

More words thrust into my broken heart like a hot sword…

"No. Impossible." I choked out the words. Trust another man?

But it *was* possible, and I realized that Mac had already taught me to trust again. To trust him.

"Esmée, you had a rough time of it. But life goes on. The war will end, and life will continue. You're young—don't give up yet."

I met his gaze then and his blue eyes sparkled like the North Sea on a summer day.

"Fine, Mac. I won't give up. You just worry about mending those bones of yours, and I'll worry about our next meal. Agreed?"

He eyed me with a mixture of amusement and something else I couldn't quite read. Compassion? Concern?

I didn't need anything to fuel the self-pity I could be prone to. Not so much since Henri was gone, but it still stole up on me like a dusting of snow in the night.

"Answer my question, Esmée. What do you want out of life?"

I sighed. "Oh, all right. I'd love to have kids, and that means I need a husband. I suppose after a time, maybe I could remarry, but for now, I…I—"

"Don't fret, Esmée. There's someone special out there for you. You don't have to know who it is yet."

His words comforted me, as though he'd stroked my hair, softly and steadily, until every worry had left my mind.

He'd touched my heart.

Chapter 6

Esmée's Journal

February 12, 1943

This may be difficult to read, since my penmanship is so shaky. It's because I'm trembling with a desire so strong I have to grit my teeth to keep from shouting my need to the world.

My need for Mac to touch me.

I pet and hug Belle often to give my hands a task other than trembling for Mac.

I treated myself to a long bath today. The first in nearly a month, and with plenty of warm water that I heated on the woodstove. It's so wonderful not to have Henri here to monitor where I spend my time and for what purpose I used the precious wood.

I washed my body and my hair with the last bits of soap I'd saved in an old silk stocking that was all but shredded from wear. The act of scrubbing off all the sweat and grime of my daily chores for the past month was liberating.

When at last the water grew cold, I stood up, toweled dry and wrapped myself in the worn woolen blanket I'd brought to the farm from my parents' home. It's bulkier than a robe but it's all I have. I went into the kitchen to boil more water. I no longer have any tea or coffee but hot water in a mug can satisfy me on these cold gray winter days.

I sat at the kitchen table with my back to the door, and looked out at the dreary day.

A noise I haven't heard in months reached my ears. The sound of a man walking. I jumped up from the table and spun around.

Mac stood in the doorway, a huge grin on his handsome face.

"I'm back on my feet, Esmée."

"Obviously. But should you be?" Worry made my voice higher-pitched than usual.

Beads of perspiration had formed on his upper lip and forehead. I prayed they weren't signs of the fever come back; just the results of his exertion. Mac was pushing himself too hard.

"Why not? It's been six weeks, and other than feeling a bit stiff, I'm able to move."

"I believe you. But you should sit and rest. Here." I pulled out the kitchen chair for him.

"I've put water on and we can sip it."

"No chance of some Earl Gray?" His question wasn't meant to be serious, as we hadn't had proper tea for years. I imagined England must have the same shortages.

"No, but the water's my own special brew." I couldn't keep the smile off my face. Mac does that to me.

"Esmée's brew it is, then." He settled into the chair and I tended to getting two cups from the cupboard behind him.

The teakettle whistled and I pulled it off the stove, careful not to get my blanket too near the flames. As I did, I suddenly realized that I was naked underneath the blanket. Mac must think I'm a harlot, I thought. But perhaps just as I hadn't noticed my state of undress, neither did he. After all, the feat of walking on one's own for the first time in six weeks was of more importance.

I poured the water and brought over the cups. I placed Mac's on the table in front of him, and moved to sit down with my own cup in the chair across from him. As I did, I stepped on a corner of the blanket and felt it tug at my arm.

I was so intent on not spilling the scalding

water on myself or Mac that it wasn't until I'd landed in my chair that I felt the cool air on my shoulders.

The blanket had fallen to my waist.

Mac's sharp hiss as he took a breath infused heat into my face, my throat, my breasts. I know I should've felt humiliation; however, I felt anything but. I yanked the blanket up, but I know Mac got a good view, to say the least.

The silence grew still and heavy between us. I waited in anticipation of Mac's next words. I couldn't speak even if I'd wanted to. I knew Mac would make some comment. I found that I was hopeful for some kind of compliment, or perhaps an invitation.

So his words took me completely by surprise.

"Esmée."

His voice trembled. I looked into his eyes.

"Esmée, I would have killed him, too, only sooner."

It took me a few seconds to understand that Mac hadn't seen me as a woman, but as a victim.

I've finally gotten the courage to look at myself in the mirror. There are several scars across my breasts where Henri whipped me with his belt, and the bruises from what I think was a broken collarbone last summer are starting to fade. They're not the usual bruises I'm accustomed to, but more like angry red bulges on my skin.

My breasts, an area of my body that should invite caresses, reminds me of the underbelly of a mangy dog. My neck appears rigid after years of anticipating the next blow from Henri's fists.

No wonder Mac didn't see me as a woman. How could any man?

February 13, 1943

I just read over yesterday's entry, not something I often do. I should be ashamed of my feelings for Mac, but I'm only human, and it's been so hard—first the war, then living with the likes of Henri. I'm not crazy; Mac's affection for me is obvious. But of course, I've been his nursemaid for the past two months. Any man would be grateful for help in the enemy's territory.

We have a love of languages in common.

When Mac speaks of his own dreams, it's difficult for me to focus on anything but him. His profile is proud and classic. Straight lines and high cheekbones.

Melinda sighed and put down the journal. It was already Tuesday, and she'd been reading Grammy's entries for the past three days straight, except for a quick break to eat or stretch.

Or to talk with Nick.

She couldn't admit, even to herself, that she was using the journal to avoid Nick.

It'd been tough enough to arrive back in their home with all the reminders of him. But to have him walk through that kitchen door— She shook her head.

She needed a change of scenery. Within five minutes Melinda had traded her slippers for all-weather walking shoes and wrapped herself in a long wool scarf over her polar fleece jacket. She knew better than to search the house for Nick; she'd heard him go off to work around seven this morning.

She had to admit she was impressed by his dedication—the fact that he'd go back right after returning from combat. He said he was easing into it, starting with a part-time schedule. She didn't think she could do it.

Melinda took a deep breath and walked down the porch steps. She had some money in her pocket; maybe she'd stop at her favorite lunch spot or at the coffee house for a mocha.

Nick glanced at his watch. Eleven-thirty. Only six more hours to stay busy until he could return to the house.

He took a swig of the water he'd switched to. Earlier, he'd downed four coffees in two hours, which only made his anxiety over Melinda tighten into an excruciating stomach pain.

Plus, it sent him to the bathroom more than he liked. Walking with his new leg wasn't as difficult as getting up and down from a seated position, especially from these soft, cushioned armchairs. Comfort had a new definition for him than before he'd lost his leg.

The bell above the door jangled and Nick looked up to see one of his colleagues, Robert Schwinn, walk in. At first Robert barely noticed him, but then recognition lit his features and he turned his full attention on Nick.

"Whoa! I didn't hear you were back in town, buddy!" Robert walked over and grabbed Nick's hand. He forced Nick up out of his chair and gave him a huge bear hug.

"We're all proud of you. Thanks for your service, man." Robert wasn't a man of platitudes, so his words meant a lot to Nick.

They sat down together and started talking business.

Just as when he'd returned from his first stint in Afghanistan, Nick's colleagues, friends and family were quick to show their appreciation for his sacrifice. Nick appreciated their support and the fact that they expressed it without hesitation.

Too bad Melinda couldn't have done the same.

Esmée's Journal
February 14, 1943

It's supposed to be a day for lovers. In any other circumstance, in any other lifetime, maybe Mac and I would be lovers. At least in my dreams.

It's foolish to trust anyone during a war, but I do trust Mac. He's been kind, despite his pain.

And patient.

I can't say I'd be so willing to allow a complete stranger to nurse me. What if I were a secret agent? Of course, I'm not.

And Mac and I are no longer strangers.

Our circumstances have nourished a special intimacy between us.

It wasn't the night in the kitchen when he saw me half-naked. It's odd, but that was the least romantic and sensual of our times together. More matter of fact. He bore witness to my scars from that man I'd spent two years with.

It wasn't a marriage. It was survival.

The most intimate times I've had with Mac haven't been when I've helped him bathe, even in the beginning when the fever kept him from doing anything for himself. It wasn't when I helped him dress, or when he caught a glimpse of me here and there, in my nightgown.

No, the most intimate time we've shared is when we talk. After the first few weeks of shock, fever and bone-mending pain wore off, Mac longed for company.

I didn't deny him, ever. I too, was eager for an adult to talk to. An adult who couldn't, wouldn't, make snide comments about my dreams or memories of a happier time before the war.

February 28, 1943

Today is the day Mac must leave. It's been more than two months now, two months of living in the same house. Often the same room, especially in the beginning.

At first I couldn't wait for him to be gone. I had to get on with my life as a widow (the neighbors all assume Henri was either taken by authorities or went to fight for the Germans). Word circulated quickly that I'd had nothing to do with any of his nefarious activities. Thank God, for to be labeled a traitor would be my final undoing.

Before Mac, I simply wanted to be able to live quietly, support the Resistance as much as possible, and feed my family what little the fields still gave me. What little Henri hadn't already given the Germans. Of course, the Germans will come for my remaining two cows soon, I've no doubt.

I dread finishing this entry, as I must get out of bed and face Mac. Will he enjoy one last breakfast with me? Or will he go without a word?

February 28, 1943

Evening entry

I helped Mac gather together a small bag of supplies. He has one change of clothes now, including the socks I knitted. He insisted on not taking more, save for a small slice of bread and a piece of moldy cheese. It was all I could scrounge up. I hate that the only clothes I have for him are Henri's. But on Mac, they don't remind me of Henri, as Mac has a lankier build.

We shared our last meal at midmorning. I hard-boiled two eggs and spread lard on toast. If it had been filet mignon and crème brûlée, it would have tasted the same—like paper.

Mac was quiet—I imagine with thoughts of what is to come. I'm sure his mind has never left his mission.

I was quiet for another reason. I will miss Mac so much. Not because I'm lonely for a man, or for company, but because *he* will be gone.

I'm afraid.

I've fallen in love with him. I have the comfort that he hasn't guessed my foolishness. Or if he has, he's never let on.

What kind of woman am I? I married a man I didn't love to save my family. When he nearly killed me and was going to kill Mac, I killed him. And here, just two months later, I'm in love with another man.

A man I don't even know, not really.

I wish I could act on the desire I feel, the desire for Mac, for his touch. I never felt this way, even before I married Henri. I've kissed my share of boys, but no more than that. None ever moved me to *want* more.

But Mac has never touched me and I want him to...

This morning I sat across from him and stared at the salt crystals that had spilled onto the wooden table. The salt was like my tears, frozen and hard inside my aching heart. I love Mac. So what? I don't deserve to feel such communion with anyone.

When at last the clock hit eleven, Mac rose and gathered his things.

"You remember the directions?"

"Yes, you've told me each day for the past week." His eyes held the barest glimmer of the twinkle I didn't know how I'd live without.

I pulled the bundle from my pocket that I'd been saving for this moment. I pressed the socks into his hand.

"Philippe will be waiting for you. Remember—"

"If he doesn't answer after three knocks, keep going until the *boucherie*." His face shone with kindness and something deeper, sadder. He held out his hand as though to touch my cheek, but stopped.

"Esmée, you are a gem."

With that, he walked out of my door and out of my life.

As I write this, I know there's no hope for the usual relief and surrender I feel when I write. This

will be part of my war records, and it will always
remind me of the sound of my heart breaking.

Chapter 7

Esmée's Journal

March 1, 1943

Mac loves me, too. I have no doubt.

How can I go from complete desolation to hope and a feeling of joy that even this bloody war can't temper?

I went to the Resistance meeting tonight. It was held in the back room of a *boucherie*. Mac left yesterday, and although I longed to ask Philippe or one of the other members where he went, I knew I mustn't. Some of my group don't even know I had Mac in the farmhouse.

We cleaned our weapons and practiced loading

them. It's a meager assortment of handguns, farm rifles and leftovers from the Great War, but it's our arsenal nonetheless. Most of us have rifles at home, as this is farm country.

As we worked, the usual talk of "outlasting" the Germans and of the Allied efforts in other countries, circulated. I saw Philippe get up and go through a small door into what I assumed were living quarters. I heard him speaking to someone, and then an answering tone I have etched in my heart.

Mac.

I knew Philippe was talking to Mac.

"Esmée, pay attention or you'll take your nail off." Jeanine's observation prodded me back from my thoughts, but only for an instant. I *had* to see Mac if he was there.

How to do this without tipping off the others?

My answer was a few steps away.

"Where are the extra cloths?"

I knew where the rags were; I just wanted my voice to be heard in the other room.

"Over there," Jeanine motioned over her shoulder. I rose and sidled behind the team of Resistance workers, to the tiny cupboard that brimmed with rags, oil-darkened brushes and small tools. I still wasn't close enough to see through the door's small opening, so I dropped a rag onto the floor and leaned over to retrieve it.

As I straightened I looked toward the door and right into Mac's eyes.

We communicate with our voices, our touch. But we also communicate with our eyes. In Mac's eyes I saw a spark of joyful recognition. So he was happy to see me, too. But then the miracle, the magic, happened. Mac's eyes became the mirror to my soul. I at once recognized need, desire, frustration and sadness.

We needed each other. We'd been forced into this situation and we desired each other as only a man and a woman can, but also as only he and I can. We were Mac and Esmée, these two people, at this particular time.

I felt as though Mac was touching me. As though his caresses played over my skin and roused my body to unimaginable heights of need. His breath seemed to scald my lips as his tongue communicated to me not verbally, but in the kiss of all kisses.

"Esmée, what's that on the floor?"

"Nothing—I just dropped the rag, that's all."

My eyes never left Mac's, but then Philippe came back into the main room and shut the door.

Shut Mac out of my life, again.

"Let's get this wrapped up. We can't linger— there are Germans in the tavern on Rue Le Havre." Philippe eyed me after he glanced around the room. Was it sympathy he showed me?

Did he see me as the war widow who's lost her mind?

Or did he sense the depth of connection between Mac and me?

Philippe had to know I couldn't have spent the last two months of my life with a man like Mac and not be affected by it.

Or perhaps he saw me as I sometimes saw myself. Coldhearted, a killer who'd murdered her own husband.

It was sheer hell to leave the meeting, knowing Mac was in the next room. I tried to convince myself that he'd already gone out another door. But my body knew he was still there. As my breath stays on a frosted windowpane after I've turned away from watching the snow fall, Mac's presence clung to me.

I bade my goodbyes and buttoned my coat before I stepped back onto the slick sidewalk. The rain is a constant this time of year. I tied my scarf tighter around my head but its threadbare condition offered little warmth against the cold and wet. I hurried along, my head down, my breathing frantic as everything in me screamed to run back to him. To Mac.

Then my head was met with a wall.

"Ouch!"

"Excuse me, madam." The German spoke poor French but I didn't care about his language skills.

I kept my head down and just stared at the buttons on his raincoat.

"Excuse me," I muttered. I took a step back so as to get away from this enemy who had his hands on my shoulders. Maybe I was lucky enough to have given him a bruise.

His fingers tightened on my shoulders. I raised my head to see his face, a full foot above mine. It was a face I knew. He was one of the bastards who'd shared a cigarette with my husband after Henri informed him where two Jewish families were being harbored in our town.

"You are the widow of Henri Breur?"

"Widow? Henri told me he had business in Brussels."

His eyes narrowed. I felt his scrutiny intensify, as did my shivers. The luxury of his raincoat was alien to me.

"Business? And how long ago was that?"

"Christmas Eve." I said the words quietly, even though my heart was ready to jump up my throat and I was afraid I might wet myself.

"Hmm. Christmas Eve. And you haven't heard from him since?"

"No, but I don't always."

Please God, I prayed, make him let go of me.

"I'll put in a word and see what I can learn. You're sure you know nothing else? You realize that lying to an officer of the Third Reich is a serious crime?"

I glared at him. It was all I could do not to spit in his face. Yet the Resistance depended on me. And Maman and Papa still needed food.

The odor of cigarette smoke mixed with winter rain stole up my nostrils as I stood in front of the German. He was used to getting his way. It was in his stance, his grip upon my shoulders and the arrogant cock of his head.

"You'd best watch your step, *Frau* Breur." He emphasized the word *Frau* so I wouldn't miss it. It's the German address for *Mrs.*, underscoring the fact that he believed Belgium to be completely under German control.

"My command headquarters is in Brussels. I can find out anything about anyone."

Good. Let him find out where Henri was pushing up sugar beets for next spring. Sugar beets the Germans would steal from us and ship home.

"Go."

He shoved me away as quickly as he'd run into me. Or rather, I'd run into him. Because my thoughts had been on Mac.

Mac.

I tried to go back to the warm place in my mind, where I was dry and the only dampness on my skin was from my desire for Mac.

I breathed a sigh of relief only after I arrived

home and rekindled the fire in the woodstove. As soon as it was hot enough, I'd boil some water to warm my bones. There was brandy in the far reaches of the storage cellar. I'd take a chance on it, no matter how old the bottle.

Anything to warm up.

Belle tagged behind me to the cellar and back up the old stone steps. She follows me everywhere now, inside and out.

Her sudden barks alarmed me.

She alerted me to the figure in the back doorway. But it wasn't an intruder.

It was Mac.

I rushed to unlock the door, each turn of the key too slow, too shaky. I released the bolt and Mac pushed open the door, then pulled me against him.

"Esmée. Forgive me, I couldn't leave without touching you."

His lips were crushed against mine.

Hot and hard.

His mouth stayed on mine for a long moment, so long that I stepped back to catch a breath. But then Mac started to move his lips over mine and I lost any chance of rational thought.

Just writing this takes me back, makes my body ache all the more for him.

He held my face in his hands and I felt the roughness of his fingertips as he caressed my cheekbones.

Our lips and tongues met with equal hunger and demand. I wanted to rip off his jacket and touch his chest, his stomach, lower.

I'd already bathed him, I knew every inch of him. Yet now I *wanted* every inch of him. And I wanted to give him every last bit of me.

For the entire time I was married to Henri, I'd never felt this way. A single kiss from Mac meant more to me than anything I'd experienced before.

I don't know how long we stayed pressed up against the open door. It was dark and still raining, and my hair hadn't dried from my walk home. The only light came from the wood fire and the tiny lamp I kept on the kitchen table.

I saw the dim light reflected in Mac's eyes when he lifted his head and looked at me.

"Esmée. I can't stay. God knows I want to."

He kept staring at me. I drank in every second of his presence.

"There are men waiting on me. I must go."

A mewling sound rose up around us. It was my own cry, my heart's protest.

"Wait for me Esmée. I promise I'll be back for you."

"Yes."

We used the next kiss to say goodbye.

The taste of Mac mingled with the salt of my tears. Maybe he cried, too. His lips played over mine as if moved by the same sorrow that clawed at my heart.

"Don't forget me, Esmée."

He kissed my forehead and pushed away. His fingers stroked my cheek, then he slipped back into the darkness.

Melinda chewed on her bottom lip. It was obvious that Mac was Grandpa Jack. Or would Grammy reveal that yet another British man had come into her life?

She knew her grandparents had loved each other deeply, but it was still a bit strange to picture Grammy as the young sensual woman her journal portrayed.

Melinda needed some distance from the story. She switched on her laptop and connected to the senator's personal network to see what she was missing. Now was the perfect time, while Nick was still at work.

Nick found Melinda at her computer with her fingers flitting over the keyboard in apparent effortless motion. His mind flashed back to when she'd spent hours working on her lesson plans or correcting papers.

"Hey, how's the journal reading?"

Melinda's body jerked in surprise. She frowned at her watch.

"I had no idea it was this late." He heard her stomach growl.

"Well, your stomach seems to know what time it is." Her lips started to curve up in a smile, until she looked at him. Until she remembered he was her enemy. Nick gripped the threshold and willed himself to remain steady.

"I have work to finish." She stared resolutely at her laptop screen.

"You won't get much done if you faint from low blood sugar. Why don't I make dinner?"

Her expression bore the wariness of a hare cornered by a lynx.

"You don't have to do this, Nick."

"I want to, Mel."

"Why?"

"I want us to be friends." *Even if we can't be anything else.*

Esmée's Journal

May 15, 1943

At last the spring air is surrounding me with physical warmth. I'd prefer the warmth of Mac's embrace, even through layers of rain-soaked clothing, to this spring sun. But it's not up to me.

I managed to plant the last of the summer vegetables. By October I should have a good crop to make some money with, or to barter for other food for Maman and Papa and Elodie.

My hands and bones ache from the farm chores, from being outside each day. But it keeps me sane. Our Resistance meetings seem to be further apart as we wait for news of liberation. Most days, I have faith it will come. As long as I'm able to coax enough eggs out of the hens and I have some hot water, I'm fine.

Where is Mac?

It's better when I don't imagine what might be happening to him. Recently the doubts have begun to filter in. Perhaps, after Henri, I would have grabbed on to anything that resembled a gentleman. No, I tell myself as I plant another root, this isn't true.

I found my mate in Mac.

It's the war that's skewed how I'm looking at it all. But if this war is what I had to live through to find Mac, so be it.

I just read over that last, and how selfish of me! Of course I don't wish this war upon us. I never have, never could. In my heart I believe the heavens would have provided a way for my path to cross Mac's. It probably would've been while I was at university, studying English literature. I would have taken a semester—or maybe even been accepted as a student!—at Oxford, and we would've met while sharing a beer over a discussion of Chaucer.

But would Mac even have noticed me, a girl from Belgium with stars in her eyes? Before the war I was so selfish and what I've done for love never would have seemed possible then. That for

Maman, Papa and Elodie, I'd marry the devil. Yet when it happened, it was as if that's how things were always meant to be.

Someone is at my door. I hope it isn't that German soldier who's been bothering me since earlier this winter.

Chapter 8

Esmée's Journal

May 18, 1943

It wasn't the German. It was Philippe. Not to inform me of a new meeting time or place.

But to bring me a gift.

From Mac.

A baby.

She's a girl with blue eyes and ringlets of chestnut hair that already surround her face at only five months. She watches my every move as though she expects me to vanish at any moment. She smells like sour milk, wet diaper and honey.

She's had a rough time of it, getting from

Ghent to here. They say she came from Germany originally, and was smuggled with her mother into Holland. But then her parents' hiding place was discovered and they smuggled her out of the house minutes before the Gestapo broke in.

Her parents are most likely in one of those death camps we've been hearing about. I pray they can survive the rest of this hell, until I can get their baby back to them. Philippe told me not to be so hopeful.

"She's yours, Esmée. Mac sent notice that the mother was in bad shape, probably typhoid or consumption, and they think the father was shot."

Melinda had to stop reading. She needed to catch her breath, which had lodged in her lungs when she read about the baby.

So Aunt Lille had been a Jewish baby. Grammy had rescued her.

"It's as though there really is a stork." She needed to hear her own voice, to confirm that she wasn't dreaming.

If only there'd been a stork for her and Nick.

According to the doctors she was fertile. So was Nick. But either their timing was off or it was simply stress that had kept her from getting pregnant. In any event, conception hadn't occurred.

Melinda shoved her feet into her boots and pulled on her coat.

Let Nicholas come home first today. She couldn't take

another day of being there, reading or making dinner, when he got home. As though she was waiting for him.

The routine was too familiar. Too comfortable for both of them.

Wet leaves stuck to her soles and she missed the crunch they'd given her yesterday. But the rain had come and now everything appeared bleak. As much as she loved autumn in New York, she dreaded the final moments, when the rain and wind took the last leaves from the branches, forming their stark silhouette for the duration of winter.

It was still daylight at three o'clock. She had about thirty minutes to pay a visit she'd needed to make since she'd returned to town.

After fifteen minutes, her walk took her through the tall wrought iron gates and along the twisting road that ran through the hundreds if not thousands of monuments that occupied East Way Cemetery. Grammy's wasn't ostentatious or religious. Just a simple, flat rectangle in pink granite.

Esmée Du Bois Busher
August 22, 1922—June 22, 2007
Wife, Mother, Patriot

A single tulip was engraved to the left of the inscription.

"Grammy, I don't understand why you didn't share

this with me sooner. It must've been an awful time, but why wait until now?"

Unexpected anger surged through Melinda.

"I have enough to do with getting through my divorce, and helping Grandpa Jack."

The rain splatted against Melinda's cheeks, and her hair began to clump.

She stood there a little longer, searching for words. For some reason she couldn't talk to Grammy at home, or in the car or anywhere—could no longer imagine her presence. But here... Her head knew Grammy wasn't actually in this grave, in the cemetery, save for her bones. Perhaps it was the finality of the grave marker, surrounded by all these other monuments; it simultaneously provided comfort and dread.

Or regret?

"I didn't mention my job, did I?" The words escaped her lips in a whisper.

"I thought it's what I wanted. I'm not sure anymore." She blinked against the burning tears.

"I'm not sure of anything anymore."

The coffee's aroma mixed with the liberal dose of chocolate syrup Charlotte had added to Melinda's café mocha.

"Jack still comes in here, you know. Same time each day."

Charlotte's turkey earrings bounced as she spoke. The café owner always dressed for each holiday, ready to give her customers a shot of cheer with their caffeine of choice.

"That's good. The routine's important for him."

"But?"

Melinda sighed.

"I'm just worried that he's not moving forward at all. And if he stays stuck here, he'll, he'll—"

She couldn't finish without tears, so she gulped her coffee instead.

"He'll go away, too." Charlotte finished it for her.

"I've watched him and Esmée come in here for over twenty years, ever since they retired. They shared a great life together, Melinda. You can't blame him for wanting to be with her, to remember."

"I don't, not at all. But I'm selfish, Charlotte. I want him here with me. Even if I can't be *here* all the time."

"Can't you move back, Melinda?"

Charlotte's brown eyes reflected her usual directness, and the question wasn't unexpected. This was a possibility Melinda wasn't ready to face.

"No, it's not something I've considered." She reached for the madeleine on the doily-covered plate of cakes.

"How does he look to you?" she asked Charlotte.

"Better. Those first few weeks were rough on all of us, but now he's speaking up more. I heard him talking about city council again, just like old times."

Both Melinda and Charlotte chuckled.

"You don't suppose he wants to run again, do you?"

"No, but if you moved back and offered to be his campaign manager, I bet he'd consider it."

"Hmm."

Charlotte was persistent when it came to making a point. Melinda used to mistake her persistence for ignorance. She knew better than to make that mistake now.

"I'm sure he doesn't need the stress of another political office."

Grandpa Jack had served in three different city-council positions over the past twenty years. He had admirers throughout the county, and his age never seemed to work against him.

Still, how much pressure could a person take?

"Melinda, your grandfather is stressed whenever he's *not* doing something."

Charlotte went to make espresso for three new customers who'd lined up. Melinda reached for more madeleines, hoping the treats would distract her from her thoughts.

Except her thoughts kept going back to Nicholas, after all.

Melinda came home to a house lit up from within. Nicholas was home. The smell of baking apple pie hit her in a wave when she entered through the back door. Now he was a baker?

He glanced up from the island butcher block.

"Hey. I hope you don't mind, but I started dinner for both of us. I took a chance that you didn't have any plans."

"Plans? No, I…"

Melinda's gaze took in the carefully set table in front of the fireplace. Burnt-orange linens and cranberry-colored candles set a festive autumnal mood. An open bottle of Bordeaux breathed on the kitchen counter.

"It's so raw outside, I figured we could use some warming up." Nick worked around the kitchen as though he'd done it his whole life. When Melinda peeked into the oven, she saw a roast.

"Is that pork?"

"Yes, and I even remembered the applesauce."

When they were first married Nick had thought it strange that Melinda refused to eat pork chops without applesauce. Then one evening they found more creative uses for the applesauce and Nick was a convert.

Melinda's cheeks burned at the sensual memory.

She looked at Nick. His eyes burned with the same memory. Suddenly the two or three paces between them felt more like two or three millimeters. Melinda drew in a breath before she spoke.

"Smells like apple pie, too."

"No, it's just a scented candle." His eyes never left hers.

Melinda willed herself to break eye contact. But she couldn't.

"Melinda." Nick said her name softly but his intent was clear.

She opened her mouth to speak in the same instant that he crossed the room. And then his mouth was on hers. Hot sensation washed over her from where his lips moved fiercely over hers down to where his palms cupped her buttocks and pressed her to him. Melinda felt dizzy, unable to breathe evenly, and her knees shook so that she had to cling to him for support.

It felt so good to anchor herself against Nick, to slip her hands around his neck, to hold his head closer to hers. She urged him to give his all to her as she stroked his teeth with her tongue.

She noticed that he adjusted his stance a bit. "Does this hurt your leg?" she murmured.

Her coat was too much of a burden between them, the kitchen too confining. Melinda wanted to be in her room with him, in her bed.

"No, no, it doesn't hurt."

"Please, Nick," she moaned against his caresses as his mouth roamed her neck and his hands worked up toward her breasts.

"Make love to me."

Nick had never felt two more polar emotions at the same time. While Melinda's hands and breath and words drove him to the edge of reason, they also served as a splash of ice water, cooling his need.

Too fast, damn it.

He couldn't risk using sex as their drug of choice for their heartache.

And he wasn't ready to tell her about his leg.

He forced his hands to still, and placed them firmly on Melinda's waist. He hated himself as he pushed her away.

"I'm sorry, Melinda. I've wanted to do that since I saw you again, but I didn't mean to be so greedy."

"It's okay." Her cheeks were flushed and her breath caught on her words. He could still take her now with no argument from her.

But not like this. Not before they'd talked everything out.

Everything.

Chapter 9

Esmée's Journal

October 16, 1943

Lille is a dream. A sweet bundle of creamy skin, silky hair and the most vivid gray eyes I've ever seen. Her eyes turned to gray about a month after she arrived.

She's starting to make sounds like words now, and she's called me *Mama*.

Mama.

I'm someone's mother!

And she was brought to me by an angel. By Mac.

God, please keep him safe. Where is he, that he was in a position to rescue this precious little one?

I love how her head rests on my chest when we lie on the couch at night in front of the woodstove. It's the warmest place in this house, and now that the autumn rains have come we spend much of our time here. She is with me always—I haven't been able to search for someone to help me. It's too risky. Besides, I can't bear to be away from her. So I keep her with me, in the sling I've fashioned out of yet another tapestry I found in the old chest in the attic.

Henri's family, or previous owners of this farm-house, must once have been rich. The tapestries in the chest are of good quality, which is obvious even though they're frayed and faded with the years.

Sometimes I feel frayed and faded, too, and yet I know that twenty-one is still young.

But I don't care about being attractive to other men anymore.

Just one man.

Mac.

October 21, 1943

Took Lille to visit the family today. Maman and Papa think I'm crazy to raise her, that I may have risked both our lives, but they also under-stand why I did it. They weren't happy about

Elodie's willingness to sign over her own identity as an unwed mother—not at first, anyway.

Elodie was thrilled to finally be able to help the Resistance effort in her own way. The polio makes any significant physical work impossible, but the doctors have always maintained that she'd be able to have her own children someday.

She agreed to sign as Lille's unwed birth mother on the forged birth certificate Philipe made up for her.

Maman wasn't without her own fears.

"Now you'll always have to continue this charade, at least until the end of the war. Just don't let Elodie get near your town for a while— they'd eat her alive."

"They" are the town gossips. I love my town, and I know that the vast majority are doing all they can to survive the war and thwart the Germans. But there's the busybody down the street who still asks about Henri; her eyebrows shot through her hairline when she saw me with Lille.

"Is looking after children one of your new occupations?" she'd asked.

"No, Madame Bousier. This is my daughter, Lille."

"I never knew you were pregnant. Quite a feat with your husband missing."

"Henri and I had always planned to adopt," I

lied. "I've adopted her from another family member who is unable to raise her.

"And why is that?"

"These are hard times for all of us, Madame Bousier."

Let her report it to the German soldier who watches over our town. He'll find only solid paperwork on my child. Thank God she has the same coloring as me—gray eyes and dark hair.

November 22, 1943

Lille took her first steps today, in front of the fire. She didn't even have to pull herself up on the furniture—she just stood and walked over to me as I ironed her linens.

These bright moments of joy give me hope that maybe the war will end sooner rather than later. That we won't have to endure another year of this hell.

It's cold and damp. The chill is bothering me more than usual.

Christmas is a month away. Another wartime Christmas.

December 1, 1943

It's wonderful to be back to these pages. I've struggled with a cough and fever. So far, Lille doesn't seem to have caught it.

Maman came over to help me after I called and told her I was ill. Thank God our phone service is still working, thanks to money from Philipe.

The German soldier showed up within a half hour of Maman. I'd like to think he followed her from the train station but I'm afraid he's been listening to my telephone conversations.

That's why Maman and I have our own code.

Maman was playing with Lille when he knocked on the front door. At least he knows his place. Only friends and family knock at the back door of a farmhouse.

"Yes?" Maman's voice was firm, her hold on Lille fierce.

"I noticed that Frau Breur hasn't been out for her usual grocery walk this past week. Is everything all right?"

"Yes. She's just come down with the flu."

"Are you here to help her?"

"Yes."

"May I see her?" His tone was cordial, almost friendly.

"No, I'm afraid not. She's resting, you see, after coughing all night."

"Nothing a shot of good brandy won't cure."

My mother made no reply. Brandy was a luxury most Belgians hadn't indulged in since before the war. She didn't mention that we had our own private stash.

I heard a small rustle.

"Here. Give her this. It will help with the cough."

Maman shut the door and locked it without another word.

Her steps sounded like those of a prison guard's when she came back to my room.

"Most German troops don't bother to bring a flask of brandy to a sick Belgian woman."

Her eyes sparked with censure and something else—fear?

"Don't worry, Maman. He's been sniffing around since Henri left and seems to have decided I'm innocent."

"He's decided you're innocent for today, Esmée. He can change his mind in a second and then you and Lille won't stand a chance."

I put down the knife I was cutting potatoes with. My hands were still shaky as I grasped the edge of the table.

"Go back to bed, Esmée. I'll finish the potatoes."

"Maman, please. Haven't I survived the worst so far?"

"It's all relative…dear."

Maman's "dear" was an afterthought, a way to

let me know she loved and trusted me, but would never trust a German soldier.

Ever.

December 23, 1943

Lille climbed the stairs today. She's a year old, and I think of how her mother must have wept at her loss. I have to watch her every step lest she hurt herself.

I'm her safety. For reasons that are still a mystery, Mac chose *me* to have Lille. He could have brought her to any number of families or couples along his route to espionage or whatever he's doing.

But he sent her to me.

I dream that she's ours, that we raise her together. In any other time or place I'd think it was foolish for me or any other woman to take a kiss and a promise as proof of a future with a man. But this is today, my beloved Belgium is still under Nazi control—at least we let the Germans think that—and I've come through a rough first marriage.

I'm not a stupid schoolgirl anymore. And Mac didn't kiss a schoolgirl. He kissed a woman. He held back nothing.

How long must I wait to feel his lips on mine again?

It's been more than ten months. It could be many more before the war is over.

Lille is crying. Must go.

Melinda awoke to the smell of nutmeg and cinnamon. She looked at the clock. 4:30 p.m. She'd been taking more naps than usual. It seemed easy to fall asleep after Grammy's entries, as though it gave her subconscious time to assimilate what she'd read.

The inky darkness that encroached early these days underscored the fact that it was autumn, normally her favorite time of year.

Why should she let this autumn be any different? Sure, she was grieving over Grammy and worried about Grandpa Jack. Oh, yeah, there was that small matter of her divorce from Nicholas.

Her cell phone, which lay on the nightstand, lit up a split second before it chimed its ring of Beethoven's "Ode to Joy."

"Hello?"

"Mel! When are you going to blow your igloo up there and get back to work?"

"Hi, Jenny. What's up?"

"Nothing since you left. I gotta tell you, I can keep the senator happy for about two more days, but then he's going to want you to do his writing again."

Jenny was the other speechwriter for Senator

Hodges. She and Melinda worked closely on most of his presentations.

"I can always e-mail you some ideas, Jen, but we agreed that these two weeks weren't a problem for anyone."

Especially me. I need this break.

"No problem at all. We just miss you."

"Have the new intern from George Washington help you. He's dying to get in on the 'real' issues."

"You expect me to substitute an overzealous college kid for you and your expertise?"

Melinda laughed. "We're all expendable, Jenny. Let me know if the senator needs me to take care of any business while I'm here." The senator hadn't been in his local office for several months.

"Will do."

When she hung up, Mel silently prayed there wasn't any local business, at least nothing complicated. She was just beginning to relax and feel like she was actually free of her usual heavy workload.

The spicy aroma that had awakened her from her nap tickled her nose again. She followed it and discovered Nick in the kitchen, standing at the stove.

"I can't get used to you cooking," she told him.

He'd never shown an interest in anything culinary before his deployments to Afghanistan.

He looked up from the carrot he was chopping and

smiled at her. The light in his eyes and the white flash of his teeth hit her like a physical blow.

"I know. It's a switch for me, isn't it? But the more I do it, the more I like it. And until I'm back at work full time, I need something to keep me busy."

"Wh-what are you making?" She took deep breaths to keep her voice from shaking.

"Chili, salad—" he nodded at the carrots "—and eggnog. It's one that involves some cooking first. I thought we could try it for dessert tonight."

"It seems early for eggnog."

"Thanksgiving's only a week away."

"Yes, I suppose it is." For the past months her days had become a blur, with no one moment distinguishable from the next.

Ever since Nick had gone to Afghanistan again. Even though she knew their marriage was doomed, she'd never been able to let go of her heart's concern for his welfare.

Rather than obsessively worry, she'd thrown herself into her work.

Of course, the day she was served with divorce papers was imprinted on her mind.

"I'm going for a walk," she told him.

"Great. Dinner'll be ready when you get back."

It took Melinda a few minutes to gather up her coat, gloves, hat, scarf and slip into her winter boots. When the door closed behind her, he allowed the smile to leave his face.

It wasn't easy, keeping up the cheerful facade. But he wanted her back. And she had to want *him* back for the right reasons. That would never happen if she found out about his leg first—he'd never be able to trust that it wasn't out of pity rather than love.

She had to want him back for the man he was, the man he'd become, for the marriage they could relish the rest of their lives.

She had to come back out of love.

Chapter 10

When Melinda returned from her walk she felt more relaxed. She took a last deep breath of the cold night air and opened the kitchen door. A blast of warmth and light hit her and she gladly soaked it up.

"Nice walk?"

"Mmm." She took in the set table, the chili bowls waiting at the two place settings.

"Nick, is this really such a good idea?"

"Probably not. But since we're going to be divorced in ten days, we need to move fast if we're going to remain friends."

"Friends? Do you think that's possible?"

"I don't know. But I think it'd be a shame to throw

away our shared history." He turned his back on her to stir the chili.

"This way, when we get remarried, we can still be friendly when we run into each other."

Nick all but choked on "remarried" but he hoped Melinda didn't notice. He risked a quick glance at her.

Her cheeks were two blotches of red, as though she'd forgotten to blend her makeup. Her lips were full and his mind kept going back to their kiss yesterday.

No repeats, man. Keep it steady.

"Shared history." She spoke the words as she took her place at the table. Nick saw that she waited for him, hands in her lap. He slid into the chair across from her. His artificial left leg hit the table and the dinnerware jumped with a clang.

"Oh! Is your leg okay?"

"I'm fine." Let her think he was a hero. She didn't know he felt nothing that struck his new limb.

"You hit the table awfully hard, Nick," She leaned to the side and started to lift the cloth.

"I'm fine," he said again. He reached across the table and clasped her other hand. He hadn't planned this physical contact but it couldn't be avoided. The last thing he needed was for her to touch his leg and find out his news now.

They'd never have a chance.

"Okay."

At his touch she straightened and that wary expression was back on her face. He withdrew his hand and grabbed his napkin.

Their touch, though brief, had been scorching.

From her silence and parted lips, he knew she'd had a similar reaction.

"Shall we?"

"What?"

"Say grace."

"Oh, of...of course."

Melinda kept her hands clasped in her lap. Nicholas said a quick prayer of thanks, then they both dug into their salads.

"Any news today?"

"With the journal?" She sighed. "Well, yes. I think I've figured out why Aunt Lille has always seemed a bit different from the rest of us."

"And why is that?"

"She was adopted."

"Really?"

Melinda went on to explain what she'd read so far. Nicholas marveled at how animated her features became when she discussed Esmée's life. The woman he'd surprised in this kitchen a week ago wouldn't have been so excited, just resigned to do what her grandmother had asked of her.

"What about Grandpa Jack's journal? Didn't you say that was with Grammy's?"

"Yes, it is." Melinda looked perplexed. "You know,

it didn't occur to me to read that yet. I thought I'd get through Grammy's first, then his."

"But maybe they were written at the same time, and you'd be able to piece together their lives more easily."

"You're right." She smiled at him as she sipped her drink. "I must admit that Grammy's story fascinates me, but the day-after-day litany of sad tales weighs on me, even though I know her life had a happy ending."

She took another sip of her water.

"She had a special dog during the war. Belle."

"At least some things were normal," he said.

And immediately regretted it.

They both fell silent.

Did Melinda remember how they'd clung together in the backyard after they'd buried Daisy? The dog who'd served as their surrogate child for their first eight years of marriage.

They'd rescued the yellow Lab mix from the pound, after she'd been abandoned on the railroad tracks nursing her umpteenth litter.

"This was great, Nicholas. Tell you what, tomorrow I'll make dinner. Would you like some tea?" She stood with her bowl and waited for his reply.

"No, thanks. I'll have another glass of wine, though, and watch the game."

"Are the Bills on tonight?"

"Not till Monday. But there's a crime show I want to watch. You gonna go read some more?"

"Yes, but I'll take your advice. I'll start tackling Grandpa Jack's side of the story."

Jack's Journal

June 15, 1943

Baby with Mum now. Enough time has passed. Did she realize I'd been listening when she talked about wanting to adopt, to save a soul?

December 21, 1943

Only three days away, walking. Can't risk any other form of transport. Wonder if this is *nuts*. Of course it is. But so am I—for Esmée and our baby. Did the little girl make it to her? Did she live?

Crazy to write this. Could hurt later. Will burn if trouble. So cold here. More sympathizers than in Germany. France is bigger than I realized. Tired of cold wet feet. Will deliver message to B.R. and get to see my love. She must understand how much I love her.

Melinda paused for a moment. "B.R." must mean Belgian Resistance.

She looked over at her laptop. E-mail had changed the face of deployment and war for her and Nick. During his first deployment, when they still wanted to

communicate, they'd been just a click of the keys away.
They'd been able to connect most days.

This last deployment, she'd avoided her personal
e-mail. Couldn't stand the "0 New Messages" statement.

Jack's Journal

December 22, 1943

Lost the day to enemy presence. Have to stay
another night in this cowshed. Farm wife kind and
thoughtful, but prudent. Didn't bring me any
food, too easy to alert nearby troops. Whispered
to me to take whatever milk I want from her cow.
Was like liquid gold, the best ale I ever tasted.
Warm, creamy, sweet. My belly aches from the
huge amount I ingested. I will tell this story to my
grandchildren someday. How God gave me milk
even in the midst of hell. But this hell will have
a good ending.
Esmée.

Esmée's Journal

December 23, 1943

Snow has covered the fields, and if the street
lamps could be on I know I'd see the fine fairy
dust of it floating down from heaven. It reminds
me of winter days when I was little and Papa
would take me for a walk down to the *patisserie*.

He'd order whatever Maman asked for: bread, warm croissants, rolls for dinner. And just when I thought he'd forgotten, he'd say, "Now, Esmée—pick out a sweet. One for you, one for Elodie." Elodie never went out with us as the cold wasn't good for her and Maman always worried about her lungs since the polio.

Today I took Lille for a walk. I bundled her in the baby clothes Maman gave me from the chest of Elodie's and my baby things. Lille is so cherubic. Her cheeks and nose poked out from her muffler, and her curls tried to sneak past the pink hat my grandmère made for me twenty-two years ago. Lille is my pride and joy. It's only been seven months but she's mine, as though she'd come from my womb.

For all the hard times and pain with Henri, she is my reward.

We went into the bakery, just as Papa had taken me. But the shelves aren't stocked full of the sweets I remember. The war has wiped us out. Madame Broussard and her husband still keep the bakery open, but the pickings are meager. Just two different kinds of loaf to choose from, the baguettes and the round ones. I know how they'll taste—more of talc than flour.

Madame Broussard greeted us as though I'd always been a widow with a baby, as though it wasn't strange at all.

"*Bonjour,* Madame Breur."

"*Bonjour,* Madame Broussard."

"And how is Lille today?"

I held up Lille for her to see, and unsnapped her hat.

"Ooh, ooh." Madame Broussard looked as delighted by Lille as I was.

"I'll have one of the baguettes, please." Then my gaze caught on something I hadn't seen for at least a year.

Fresh Belgian chocolate pralines.

Madame didn't miss anything.

"Perhaps a few treats for your Christmas stocking?"

I opened my mouth to protest; I couldn't afford even one of them. But my mouth watered as if my tongue could taste the rich concoction, if only in my imagination.

But Madame Broussard wasn't talking to me. She was talking to Lille—and didn't she put three chocolates in a small bag? She then placed the bag next to the baguette and wrapped it in the dishtowel I'd brought for the baguette.

"*Joyeaux Noel,* Lille." Gazing at Madame, I saw a twinkle that could have been from Saint Nick himself.

"*A vous aussi.*" Smiling at Madame, I placed

Lille's hat back on and walked out of the shop, the parcel firmly nestled in my gloved palm.

"It's awfully cold to have a baby out on the streets, Esmée." The German soldier blocked my view as he stood in our path.

"She's dressed warmly enough and the fresh air does her good." I kept my tone light. This Nazi didn't take to heavy tones from any Belgian, but especially a woman.

"Tsk tsk." He clucked his tongue against the roof of his mouth and I saw him lick his lips afterward. I averted my gaze. Anything to quell the nausea that rose in a huge wave each time I ran into him.

"Call me Johan." His request was a command, but not one I'd ever follow.

"That's a bit familiar, isn't it?" I plastered a smile on my lips and held tightly to Lille. She started to whine and wiggle. Neither was usual for her.

"We're hardly strangers. I brought you brandy when you were ill."

"Yes, you did. Thank you very much. Now I must go." He allowed me to pass, but put his hand on my arm.

"Merry Christmas, Esmée."

I kept on walking. I couldn't return his Christmas greeting. As I walked home, I hoped he wouldn't follow, and wouldn't bother me during the holiday.

Jack's Journal

December 23, 1943

Stuck here. All I can think about is Esmée.

I knew while the barrel of that gun was still hot that she was mine. The one I was destined for. It may seem odd to fall in love with a woman who's just killed her husband, but she had her reasons. She saved my life.

Those scars on her body. I want to kill the son-of-a-bitch all over again. Make him suffer for what he's done.

Glad I saw her at the Resistance meeting or I would've wondered this entire time if she cared for me as I did her, or if she was just vulnerable from her bad experiences.

Risky to go back to her house but I had to. I had to show her the only way I know how that she's connected to me and that I won't forget her. Our bond isn't one of these hasty wartime couplings. It's crazy, it's nuts, but it happened. I fell into the pasture of an angel.

When I kissed her, she didn't hold back one bit. We could have made love right there on the threshold of her old farmhouse.

But she's too special for that. What we have is too special. I will go back for her as soon as I'm able and finish what we started.

Melinda found the style of Grandpa Jack's entries confusing at first. She supposed he kept lots of things vague in order to protect anyone mentioned in his journal. Even the way he wrote Grammy's name, with the "E" resembling an "H" and the entire word looking more like Helen than Esmée was obviously another layer of protection.

She wondered if she would've had the presence of mind to write in a pseudo-code. Of course, Grandpa Jack had been trained for any type of wartime scenario.

Had Nick thought of her in the same way while he was gone?

A giggle tried to escape at the thought. But it turned into a sob.

Of course he hadn't.

Chapter 11

I wasn't praying for this. I was doing my best to be grateful this Christmas. I have my health. Maman and Papa and Elodie are well. I wish I had more to give them, but at least none of us have starved during this horrendous war.

I kept trying to stay focused on that during Mass last night. On how I'd travel to Maman and Papa's and take the chicken we'd roast for dinner. I'm lucky I had chicks last spring. I've been able to have chicken every now and then, for a treat, or when I feel Lille needs the nourishment.

I swear I wasn't asking God for anything else, just my family safe, and maybe a hint that Mac is still safe, wherever he is.

I tried my best not to wish for anything grander.

Yet, just as God sent Gabriel to Mary, He sent me Mac.

One thing that even the war can't stop is love. I love Mac, and he loves me. But what we share is so much greater than either of us. I wish I could claim credit, feel that I've earned this. But I haven't, nor do I deserve it.

I am so blessed. Mac and Lille and I are blessed.

Will write more tomorrow.

December 26th 1943

He came as softly as the new-fallen snow, but before he left this morning we'd experienced a blizzard of emotions.

The war has taught me that a lifetime can no longer be measured in normal days, months or years. Someone can turn from an innocent young child to a hardened criminal with one explosion, one bullet.

So I no longer find it strange that Mac and I have found each other and that there's no doubt in my heart, my soul, or even my mind—which remains ever-pragmatic—that we are soulmates. I would travel to the ends of the earth to be with him, and he has traveled from the ends of the earth to be back here with me and Lille on our first anniversary. The first anniversary of when we met, grotesque though it was.

He was waiting for us after Mass.

Lille and I went to Midnight Mass. I'd decided earlier in the week to stay here in town, and Maman and Papa agreed. Lille and I could go on Christmas Day to see them.

But Lille and I never left the house on Christmas.

We had the most pleasant reason to remain at home.

"Come, come, *ma petite*. It's warmer inside." Lille wriggled in my arms as we walked home after Mass. Since she started walking, she rarely allows me to hold her for more than a few minutes. This often makes our outings much longer but never boring.

She'd used up her patience in church.

"Non, non, non, Maman!" Lille stopped to look at each flake of snow, each blade of grass that still poked through the crusty white layer.

"Lille, it's the coldest winter yet but you're happy to stay outside and have us both freeze." I wanted to scoop her up and hustle her the rest of the way home, but her shrieks drew too much attention.

"*Joyeux Noel*, Esmée."

"*Bonsoir.*" So much for keeping Lille quiet. Now I had to deal with the German soldier again.

I was grateful for the cover of night so he couldn't see my face very clearly.

"It's cold tonight, Esmée. You shouldn't be alone on a night like this."

"I'm never alone."

I gathered Lille into my arms.

"Come, Esmée. Not all of us are Gestapo. What are you afraid of?" His gloved hand touched my chin and tilted my gaze to his.

"I'm not afraid of anything. I have a busy life."

Lille buried her head against my shoulder. Not typical for her, but even an infant knows trouble, no matter how smoothly it's dressed.

Did he suspect I was with the Resistance? There'd been rumors that the Germans were frustrated with the advances of the Allies and therefore looking for Belgians to take their frustration out on. Especially suspected Resistance.

Lille's high-pitched shriek crackled the air around us.

"*Pardon.* I must be on my way." I bundled her closer to me.

His laughter followed me. "One day, Esmée, you'll realize what you've given up."

Another opportunity for murder is all I'm giving up, I thought.

We arrived home at last. I'd left a tiny fire going in our bedroom, just for tonight. It didn't give off much heat but it was enough to make the house seem a bit cheerier than normal.

I threw in some wood and got Lille ready for bed.

"Non, Maman, non." I laughed as she ran away from me, naked, not wanting the confines of her nightgown.

"Remember St. Nicholas day?" I cajoled. "Tomorrow will be just like that. You might find some sweets when you wake up!"

It took two lullabies and more stories than usual, but after an hour I finally settled Lille down to sleep.

I went out to the back to gather some more wood before I prepared for bed. There was more than wood waiting for me. Belle walked protectively at my side. She let out a sudden whimper and her tail thumped against my leg.

"Mac!"

The bundle of wood fell from my hands and my heart skipped two beats.

He was alive! My worst nightmares were cancelled out as I stared at this man who'd helped me through the most difficult time of my life. And provided me with my life's dream in the process.

His face was the same, just thinner. His clothes were tattered and dirty. He looked like the peasant he no doubt wanted to resemble. But his eyes were all mine. And his hair, his rich, thick hair.

"Esmée." We stood in the yard for what was probably only a few minutes but could have been hours. Our eyes once again communicated all that had passed since our last meeting.

Since our first and last kiss.

I saw joy, regret, relief, hope in Mac's eyes.

What he saw in mine, if they reflected my heart, would have been surprise, joy and love.

Belle whined again and kissed his hand, and that broke the spell.

"It's so cold out here. Please, let's go in." I stooped to gather up the logs and Mac was there, his hands strong and sure as he helped me.

"How is the girl?" The kitchen door closed behind us.

"She's so beautiful, I—" I couldn't answer him as the tears sprang to my eyes. Instead, I motioned for him to follow me.

Lille's crib was next to my bed in the main bedroom. The fire I'd started earlier still glowed in the old fireplace and cast an angel's lighting around Lille. The air smelled sweet as if touched by her baby's breath.

"Oh, Esmée." Mac was mesmerized by the child.

Our child.

"She's our baby girl, Mac."

"Are you sure, Esmée?" His eyes were on Lille's still form.

"Yes."

"She sleeps so peacefully." His voice trembled with wonder. How many months, years, since *he'd* slept like that?

"It's been a long day for her. We played outside in the snow. Fresh air—"

Mac's hand grabbed mine and he pressed his fingers to my lips. His touch was at once warm, soft, insistent.

Exciting.

A slow roil of warmth clutched my belly and spread lower until I thought I'd melt with longing.

"Can we leave her here to sleep?" Mac still held my hand.

"Of course."

Two minutes later, we were in front of the kitchen woodstove. Mac tugged on my hand and I answered by throwing myself against him. We looked at each other.

One last look before we gave into months of unexpressed passion and desire.

His mouth insisted on nothing less than my total surrender. His hands touched not just my clothes, then my skin, but also my heart as he showed me his own.

I was used to being a release for a man. I wasn't used to being made love to and that's exactly what Mac was doing. This first time we were more like animals, wild in our need, but Mac treated me as though I was so precious, so beautiful.

As though I deserved to be loved.

"I love you, Esmée." His words poured over me like honey on warm bread. I opened my mouth to his tongue, my body to his touch, my heart to our union.

I wish I could describe our joining in more detail but words can't do it justice.

Besides, I was so dizzy with need I'm not sure I'd remember everything!

Later, we lay on the blanket and reveled in our nearness. Skin against skin.

"I've wondered where you were each day," I whispered.

"I felt your thoughts. They brought me back to you."

"Are you finished with your mission?" Why did I ask him this? I knew the answer.

"No, not until—"

"Until the war is over."

"Yes."

"How soon do you think it will be, Mac?"

"Soon. But it will be rough until the liberation. The Germans won't go down easily."

"They have no choice."

"They've doubled their patrols on the borders. It's impossible to go back and forth."

"Yet you did?"

He sighed and rubbed my thigh.

"Yes. For this." He pressed my palm to his lips. "For you."

"I'm so glad you're here. But how will you get back?"

"The Resistance will get me out again. I had to come back to report on the activity in France, as well. To help keep up morale."

"It's so hard to know we're so close to winning and yet…"

"I know, Esmée. You must be strong. For Lille. For us. For our life after the war."

"You believe we'll make it, don't you?"

"I have no doubt. "

"Will you come back here after it's over?"

"I don't know, Esmée. Of course I'll come back for you and Lille. But I don't think I could live here after the war. What about you?"

He'd stated my thoughts aloud.

"I don't want to stay here anymore, either. I'll miss Maman and Papa and Elodie, but the memories here…" I shivered in spite of the heat our passion cast around us. "Even in a new home, I'm afraid I'd forever see the German troops marching, or Henri talking to them."

"We could have a new life in America."

"America?" I thought for sure he'd say "England."

"I could get a teaching job in the United States. And your fluency in languages would help you find work, too. You could continue your education if you'd like."

I laughed. "But I have our daughter to raise."

"So? Can't her mother go back to school?"

"You said you teach."

"In my real life I'm an English professor. Oxford."

"Oxford? I'd hoped to study there after I obtained my degree!"

"Oh, Esmée, I'm sorry. The war has ruined many dreams, hasn't it?"

"Not the most important." I snuggled deeper against him, and placed his hand on my breast.

"No, my love, not the most important."

His lips caressed the back of my neck and my desire rose with such ferocity I had to remind myself to breathe.

The second time, and each time thereafter, was more reverent, slower. As though we savored every taste, touch and kiss. The firelight and the dim bulb in the corner of the room threw shadows on the walls and I saw our bodies merge into one shape, one form.

No longer a war spy and a Resistance worker, we were Esmée and Mac.

We were one.

At some point during the night, he told me his real name, and where I'd find him in America after the war if he didn't make it back here. If I was able to travel before him, he would meet me there.

We agreed to start over again, together.

Chapter 12

Esmée's Journal

March 11, 1944

The saddest event today. Philippe was murdered by the Gestapo. Someone gave away our meeting place. He was taken out and shot in the middle of the street, in the middle of our quiet town. Thank God I wasn't there with Lille. My neighbor, Herbert, told me out in the field as he tended his henhouse and I fed Lait. She's been a good milk cow all these years. And I have plenty of eggs. I can only hope they'll last until the liberation.

The BBC reports Papa and Maman tell me

about must be true. The end is near. What other explanation for such a sweep of the Resistance this late in the game? The enemy is most desperate before surrender.

I have a strong urge to flee for safety, but of course, it's impossible until we're liberated.

My hands aren't very steady as I write. I spoke with Philippe just two days ago. He looked more tired, more haggard than usual. Of course, the war has worn on all of us. Even with the food in the countryside, we don't have enough. Plus the constant worry…

I saw Philippe at the cemetery. We use it as a sort of checkpoint among ourselves. We're never seen talking there. Just visiting our family gravesites. But we have hand signals we've developed. So far, the Germans haven't noticed us. Not to my knowledge, anyway.

Philippe didn't have to use hand signals, though. He was one row behind me and Lille, to the left.

I'd been gazing at the tomb of someone I don't know. Anything to occupy my mind, which continues to race with what ifs.

"Don't look behind you, Esmée." I recognized his soft voice.

"Okay." Still, I chanced a quick look around—no one was there that I could tell. Just rows and rows of tombstones.

"I'm sorry to tell you—the devils got him."

I swayed. I clutched Lille tighter to me, fighting the pain that seared my heart.

"No, no." He meant Mac. The devils referred to the Gestapo.

"He had a job over there and got arrested with some star families."

"Over there" could mean anywhere else that's occupied, but most likely Germany or the Netherlands. "Star families" meant Jews.

"Oh, dear God, no!"

"I'm sorry to tell you."

I heard footsteps crunch on the gravel pathway. Philippe stood in the row in front of me now, his head tilted as though he was looking at a tombstone. But his intense gaze was on me.

"You mustn't despair. He's a hero, and if anyone can survive the mess he's gotten into, he will. You must keep on for him, for all of us. You know, when he left your place at Christmas, they almost got him. But we changed his clothes and he escaped. He's a survivor."

Tears stung my eyes but what could I say to this man who'd already risked so much to fight the enemy in our own backyard?

"I'll never give up," I vowed.

We stared at each other a bit longer. I felt we were giving each other strength with that gaze. He nodded.

"Good girl," he said in a low voice. He meant me, not Lille.

Lille had been surprisingly quiet but started to squirm in my arms. The cold damp of the Belgian spring bothered her, even though I'd wrapped her well.

I adjusted her hat, whispering sweet talk to her. When I looked back up, Philippe was gone.

I cast my gaze over the abandoned cemetery.

"This isn't a place for us, Lille, nor for your papa." For the father of the baby who grew inside me.

Mac.

We weren't destined to die and be buried here.

I'm writing this by candlelight. That's nothing new, except for the fact that Lille and I are no longer free to move around. It's necessary to avoid the Germans and informants. I'm so afraid we'll die in the camps we keep hearing about.

The German soldier dealt me my final hand after I'd spoken to Philipe in the cemetery.

The pounding at the door woke me at five. I'd been in a deep warm slumber. I was with Mac in my dreams, as always.

My heart pounded in time with the pounding at the door.

I moved the heavy curtain over the door window and gasped. Seeing the German in uniform at such an early hour raised every hair on my neck, my arms.

I opened the door.

"You see what we do to Resistance, Esmée?" He held Philippe by his collar. Blood still poured from his swollen wounds.

"My God." I choked on the words and forced the nausea down.

"Don't make the same mistake."

I didn't say anything. Bit my lips to quell the screams that wanted to escape.

"I'll be back later, Esmée. I can make life so much easier for you." He stared at me for a minute. I didn't back down from his stare, but I wanted to slam the door in his face and run for Lille.

My baby!

I saw him reach over into his passenger seat. He threw something out the window.

Finally he screeched off and left me standing there in the still, cold morning.

What he'd thrown out his window drove me to my knees. Even in the dark I could tell what it was.

"No!" I screamed into the dawn air.

On the ground where he'd dropped it lay Mac's jacket. Soaked in blood.

After I'd retrieved it, I locked myself back in the house. I made myself calm down. Think.

I looked through the jacket. My picture was in there. One taken just before the war. It had been on my bureau. Mac must have taken it as a re-membrance. It was a tiny black-and-white portrait I'd never noticed was missing.

Of course—Philippe had Mac's jacket. From what Philippe told me yesterday, he'd saved Mac's life when Mac was leaving me and Lille at Christmas. The Germans had almost got him then. But Philippe had taken Mac's jacket and put him in an old man's outfit instead.

He'd saved Mac's life.

I knew on some level that Mac was most likely dead. Or at least the enemy thought he was. Otherwise the German wouldn't have left me alone while he finished off Philippe.

I have to keep going. I have to believe, for Lille and me. I can't imagine life without Mac. He is my life. He's Lille's father, our baby's father.

Now I'm living for both Lille and Mac. For all of us.

Friday, one week after her return home, was Melinda's favorite kind of Buffalo day. Cold, yes, but nothing her parka and cashmere scarf couldn't handle. The sun was as bright as it'd get in the November sky, and the remaining leaves that hadn't been blown away by last week's snowstorm floated to the ground. The snow had melted and she wondered if they'd have a white Christmas. Still a month away. They could have three feet by then.

She was grateful for the convenience of their neighborhood. She walked to the library, a fifteen-minute jaunt from home. In worse weather she'd have to take the car but today the walk was perfect. No threat of rain or snow with the light wispy clouds that framed the bare branches of the trees.

Melinda could have used her laptop at home, but she couldn't risk Nicholas walking in on her. She needed to learn what she could about his stint in Afghanistan without his thinking she was spying on him.

It was silly. She could just ask him.

But the Internet wasn't personal.

The library smelled, as it always did this time of year, of books and damp coats. Melinda smiled at the librarian at the front desk, a new woman she didn't recognize.

"I need an Internet computer, please."

"Can I have your driver's license?"

Melinda handed over her ID, trusting the woman didn't know her or her family.

No such luck. "You're Esmée's granddaughter?" The woman's blue eyes darkened with compassion.

"Yes. You're good—my maiden name isn't on there."

"Esmée was always talking about you and your husband, Nick."

"And you're?"

The woman let out a self-conscious giggle. "I'm sorry. I'm Alice Shapinski. I moved back from California last year, and your grandmother was wonderful to me."

Melinda racked her brain for a memory of this woman at the funeral. Nothing came to mind.

"Nice to meet you, Alice."

Melinda stuck out her hand. She hoped Alice was really a friend and not someone who collected facts on the area and its inhabitants.

"I'm sorry we didn't meet at the funeral. I was in the back during Mass, but I couldn't bring myself to go to the cemetery. Your grandmother was very special."

"Yes, she was."

Melinda put Alice close to her own age.

"What sent you out to California?"

"The same thing that sends us all, I suppose. I wanted to see the world, find the opportunities I thought I was missing here. I went to UC Berkeley, then worked in California library systems for ten years. I got my Master's while I was out there, too."

"So what brought you back?"

"It's more like 'what drove me away from California.'" Alice's smile grew tremulous and Melinda hoped she wasn't going to start crying.

What was it with women her age?

"A man?"

"Yeah." Alice lifted her chin and drew in a shaky breath. Her fuzzy pink angora sweater trembled. Alice might have been hurt by a man, but not enough to keep her from dressing to attract another.

Including the glossy come-kiss-me lipstick on her lips.

"Now that I'm back, I have no doubt it was the right choice. I'm able to help out my folks if they need me, and I've been spending more time with my nieces and nephews."

Melinda smiled at Alice. "I wish I had nieces and nephews. I'm getting too old for kids of my own, and it would be nice to have younger children in the family."

She didn't count Nicholas's brother's kids as her own anymore. She couldn't afford to.

"Too old? No way, girlfriend! We're the same age—" she nodded at the driver's license "—and I know my eggs may be ripe but they're still worth plucking!"

Melinda couldn't stop the laugh that crept out of her throat. This gal was too much. Alice represented exactly what Melinda had wanted to leave behind when she went to D.C.

The hope for a future filled with love.

"I've distracted you," Alice said. "You're at computer K. If you need anything, let me know. Of course, from what Esmée told me, you could teach me a thing or two about the Internet."

"My grandmother was always wearing rose-colored glasses when she looked at me."

"I wouldn't be so quick to say that." Alice smiled at Melinda, then turned her attention to the next person in line.

Melinda escaped to the confines of the computer

room. She wasn't happy that the computers were all along a wall and anyone could come in and peer over her shoulder, but it was still safer than at home.

Besides, she knew the librarians had their hands full monitoring the teenagers, among others, preventing them from surfing not just porn but terrorist and other dark-subject Web sites. She'd worked thirty-three eighteen-hour days in a row last summer to push through legislation that the senator supported on safe Internet access in public libraries.

She smiled to herself as she acknowledged the irony of having worked on that critical piece of legislation. She was going to use everything she'd learned about the Internet to make sure her own digital fingerprints were absent from her search.

Melinda scrolled through several Web pages of newspaper articles. All she'd been able to find on Nick's unit was that three members were injured, one killed last May by an IED. Not an uncommon occurrence.

Was this the incident that had caused his leg injury?

Who was the soldier who'd died? Nick hadn't mentioned any of this to her.

If he'd gone through anything unusual, she wouldn't find it via public records.

She'd have to delve deeper.

In all likelihood, Nick had removed her from his next-of-kin notification. She doubted she was still on his Page Two, the sheet in his service jacket that designated his military life-insurance beneficiaries.

And he'd never indicated that he'd given her contact information to his unit's Family Readiness Group.

Her gut ached. A sure signal that it was time to ask the source himself.

Nick.

Esmée's Journal

September 7, 1944

James came into this world just as Belgium was liberated from the Germans. Finally, an end to our suffering. At least of the worst kind.

Both sides tried to get in their final, merciless blows. Several Germans came to our town three days before our liberation and routed out Resistance members, whom they executed. To have made it so far, to be so close to freedom—and murdered in such a brutal fashion.

My friend from high school, Marie, was discovered dead, her throat slit. I thought that news would send me into labor. But since I knew she'd been fooling around with a few of the German soldiers, and one in particular, this wasn't a surprise. I never thought of her as an actual traitor, but then again, why did she have to tempt fate?

It's such a relief to see that the Resistance work has succeeded. Still, so many of my colleagues were executed point-blank by the Germans, especially over the past couple of years. Dear Philippe.

Our meeting place was discovered and he was the only one in it. He refused to give up any of our names. Although my involvement was less after I had Lille, and certainly once I became pregnant, I still did whatever I could.

On the occasional train ride into Brussels, I'd pass a message to another Resistance member. I looked like any other wartime mother with Lille on my hip or in the ancient pram I found for her up in the rafters of our old barn.

Once I was pregnant I had to be more careful. My clothes were quite loose on me, which was a godsend, for my blossoming stomach didn't show for many, many months. But these last two months, I've worried. It's been so difficult, knowing the end is close and yet the end of my life and that of my children could come at the whim of one beleaguered German soldier.

Thank God our local Gestapo soldier left in May. Said nothing, just wasn't here one day. When I recall how I was afraid I'd have to flee with Lille, and James in my belly, it makes me sick.

No time for that today. Today I am the mother of two babes. Lille and James, who arrived last night. I started feeling out of sorts yesterday morning. Maman came to help the midwife. I had more bleeding than normal, according to the midwife. She told me that my womb wasn't contracting as quickly as it should and encouraged me to nurse James as much as possible. I thought of Mac all the while I was in labor. I thought I'd hear from him. Last month, after Paris was liberated, then most of France, and now, Belgium.

But no word.

His mission probably took him into the heart of this mess, but surely he's not still in Germany? I pray he was never there, that Philippe was wrong.

I know it's not just my emotions getting the best of me. Mac and I are destined for each other, no question. He loves me, and I him. Our love is greater than both of us. Just look at James!

He has Mac's hair, all waves and chestnut-colored. Maman said she's never seen a newborn with such a head of hair. Both Elodie and I were bald until age two.

James is content to nurse, be swaddled and quietly held. He doesn't like to be put down at all. It's as though he somehow feels the absence of his father.

Mac, Mac, you must come soon. You must see your son. Philippe was murdered before I could use him to get word to Mac about my pregnancy. I have no other contacts who could do so, and even if I did it would've been too dangerous. I imagine it will get easier to move around and travel over the next months as the Germans surrender.

James, I want you to know that you were born to a people and a nation who never capitulated. We took our occupation with the dignity only God can give us, and with supernatural strength, in my opinion. The blessed Allies came in and saved us like angels from heaven, but they couldn't have done it if we hadn't been waiting and willing to be freed.

Ahh, I hear my baby calling for his milk. My breasts are swollen and I can feel the milk coming in as he cries.

I long to share this with Mac.

December 26, 1944

Yesterday was my last Christmas in Belgium. It's time to follow through our dream, Mac's and mine. I'll make sure he can reach me, find us, if he comes back here or tries to call. But I have to go.

Maman doesn't understand. Not at all.

"You can't travel around the world with two infants. It's impossible." Her hands shook as she fussed with Lille's dress. James suckled at my breast.

"Maman, these children deserve to have a father. Here they'll always be questioned, thought of as illegitimate. In America we can start anew."

"What makes you think you can provide for

yourself and your children? You don't really believe this Mac will show up, do you?"

"I have my languages to support us. And I have no doubt Mac will find us. He's done something very important for the war, Maman. Because of brave men like him we were able to be liberated."

"You haven't heard from him in a year, Esmée." Maman was tough, I'll give her that. She'd never expressed disapproval over my pregnancy or my love for Mac. But then, she'd always been a practical woman.

"Maybe he made it over to America first and hasn't been able to get in touch with us." My reply sounded fantastical, delusional. But my heart knows the truth, and the truth is that Mac lives. There is a reason we haven't been reunited. A logical reason.

"How will you get over there?"

"I have some money from the old things I've sold out of the attic." Items that were part of Henri's family, or the previous owner's. But I didn't part with all the tapestries.

"And the earnings from selling the farmhouse?" Maman's raised eyebrow said it all. She didn't think I'd ever sell the old building. Not this soon after the war.

"I'm not selling it. I'll rent it out." What I didn't tell her is that I'm not renting the old house. I'm giving it to Elodie. She's fallen in love with a Belgian Resistance agent and they'll be married by the end of winter. But she needs to tell Maman and Papa in her own time. So I said nothing.

"Belle can stay with you. Elodie will enjoy that." What it really meant was that Belle could live out the rest of her days on the farm.

"I'll find Aunt Esther, like we wanted to before the war." My maternal grandmother's sister had gone over nearly thirty years ago and had offered to sponsor us as immigrants but we'd never thought it was necessary.

Until it was too late.

Maman was sad but resigned to my plan. She understood because I am, after all, her daughter.

Chapter 13

September 6, 1945

They told me I have to start this journal. That I should write to free my heart of these chains. "They" are my sister, Pauline, her husband, Bob, and Reverend Tom. I just call him "Tom." After baring one's soul of the most horrendous sights and sounds, it's hard to call anyone "father."

It's been nearly a year since they freed us. Since the Allies came, my own Brit brothers. I've finally put on a few stone, but I have more to gain if I'm ever to become the man I was.

Silly thought, that. I'll never be the man I was.

I must admit it's freeing to be able to write normally again, not just in my own pseudo-code.

October 4, 1945

My bones ache and my hands tremble as I write. The fever has come back. The doctors have prescribed antibiotics and assure me that one day I'll wake up and never have another. Yet when the fever comes on, it's fast and furious and the familiar pain threatens to swallow me whole. This is better than when I had fevers in the camp, though. There I slept on the floor so as to cool myself off. The bug and rodent bites were worth it.

If I thought these fevers would rid me of my nightmares I'd give in to them. But I never want to lose the memory of the sweetest thing my life ever knew. Esmée. Esmée and Lille. Lille is over two years old now. She wouldn't recognize me.

Would Esmée? She's made no apparent attempt to locate me. Of course, I haven't been able to go back to Belgium, not as I am now. I could ask my sister to send a letter for me, or try to call someone in her town. But it's not right.

Esmée deserves more. I can't be a man to her and father to Lille when all I am is a burden to whomever I stay with. I'm so grateful to Pauline for taking me in.

It's been difficult learning that Mum didn't survive the war. She died in a bombing, when Dad was out getting a loaf of bread. It's ironic that he was above ground and lived, and she, in her basement kitchen, was crushed under the weight of the apartment building.

Why didn't she come out to Pauline's here in Kent? Not that it would've felt any safer, but surely it was preferable to London.

October 15, 1945

It's been exactly six months since I could see an end to my hell. It wasn't a bright light that shone all at once. I find it painful to think about, worse to ignore it. The monsters don't leave me alone. I have to face them, like the doc and the reverend say.

I need to get well for the same reason I survived this past year—Esmée.

I was finishing up what would've been my sixth successful mission as an SOE agent. Ever since the RAF dropped me from that Whitley into Esmée's pasture, I did my best to catch all the rest of my rides with the same squadron in a Lysander. Not the prettiest plane ever built, but it can land and take off from the worst field imaginable, all in a few minutes.

Dutch Resistance told me my ride would be at

point Delta, a farm field several miles from where I'd been gathering information on the most recent activity conducted by the Gestapo in and around Amsterdam. It was February 1944. I'd left Esmée and Lille in their warm home and ventured north, hoping to finish my part in the war. Hoping to see Northern Europe liberated.

I didn't expect the raids. None of us did. Scores of Jewish families who'd remained hidden until now were being rounded up and hauled off. The brave citizens who'd sheltered them were hauled off, as well, if not shot on the spot.

I was betrayed. The Resistance contact man I usually did business with didn't show up in the cemetery where we usually met. Instead, a stranger. He said all the right things, knew all the code words, but my gut told me something was wrong.

I decided to get to the Lysander landing site an hour earlier than scheduled. If it wasn't there that night, I knew the protocol—come back again the following night, and then the following, until it showed up.

I took the usual precautions as I left the barn loft I'd been sleeping in. I was certain no one saw me leave the farm, nor was I spotted on my walk out to the country.

But the traitor must have followed me back the night before. Maybe he'd been keeping tabs on me the whole time.

As I lay on my belly in a rut and contemplated whether Dutch soil was colder than Belgian, I felt the crushing blow between my shoulder blades.

A kick to my shoulder flipped me over before I could catch my breath.

"Traitor."

It was the so-called Resistance agent I'd met yesterday.

As I looked up at him, I heard the first drone of the Lysander's engine. It was early. I had about two minutes to deal with this buffoon, then get on the plane.

Did he think I was Dutch? He didn't know I was SOE?

I opted for the most direct approach.

"Go to hell."

"No, you're the one who'll burn in hell." He lifted his leg to kick me again. I grabbed his foot and with one move had him on his back.

I'd always taken my hand-to-hand training seriously, and it stood me in good stead throughout the war.

I was on top of him now, my hands around his neck.

"Tell me who you are. Who do you work for?"

"Never." His eyes started to bulge with the pressure of my hands on his windpipe.

I let up the pressure just enough.

"Talk!" The sound of the Lysander tempted me but I had to take care of this distraction.

"I know you're Gestapo." He coughed as he sputtered out the words.

"What? What's your game, fool?" I had my grip back around his neck.

"I heard you talking to the soldier last week. You were in a uniform."

I relaxed my hands. He sounded like a native Dutch speaker, and the information he'd given me yesterday could only have come from true Resistance channels. My hackles had risen because I must've picked up on his mistrust of me.

"Yes, you did, you idiot. I was undercover. How else do you think we gather information on the enemy?"

His bloodshot eyes looked at me, still suspicious.

"If you're undercover, then what other languages do you speak?"

"It doesn't matter. Why did you give me the correct time?"

"So I'd find you out here." As he spoke, the Lysander's engine rang like music to my ears. "I thought you were going to sabotage the aircraft. I planned to take you out."

I looked up and saw that the plane had touched down approximately four-hundred yards to the west of us. I knew it would wait only long enough to ID me and take me aboard.

The Harlequin Reader Service® — Here's how it works:

Accepting your 2 free books and 2 free gifts places you under no obligation to buy anything. You may keep the books and gifts and return the shipping statement marked "cancel." If you do not cancel, about a month later we'll send you 4 additional books and bill you just $4.47 each in the U.S. or $4.99 each in Canada, plus 25¢ shipping & handling per book and applicable taxes if any.* That's the complete price and — compared to cover prices of $5.25 each in the U.S. and $6.25 each in Canada — it's quite a bargain! You may cancel at any time, but if you choose to continue, every other month we'll send you 4 more books which you may either purchase at the discount price or return to us and cancel your subscription.

*Terms and prices subject to change without notice. Sales tax applicable in N.Y. Canadian residents will be charged applicable provincial taxes and GST. Credit or debit balances in a customer's account(s) may be offset by any other outstanding balance owed by or to the customer. Please allow 4 to 6 weeks for delivery. Offer available while quantities last.

Play the Lucky Hearts Game

and get...

2 FREE BOOKS and
2 FREE MYSTERY GIFTS...

yes! YOURS to KEEP!

I have scratched off the silver card. Please send me my **2 FREE BOOKS** and **2 FREE mystery GIFTS**. I understand that I am under no obligation to purchase any books as explained on the back of this card.

Scratch Here!
then look below to see what your cards get you... 2 Free Books & 2 Free Mystery Gifts!

353 HDL ENT9   153 HDL ENMX

FIRST NAME	LAST NAME

ADDRESS

APT.#	CITY

| STATE/PROV. | ZIP/POSTAL CODE | (H-E-11/07) |

Twenty-one gets you
2 FREE BOOKS and
2 FREE MYSTERY GIFTS!

Twenty gets you
2 FREE BOOKS!

Nineteen gets you
1 FREE BOOK!

TRY AGAIN!

"Because of your mistake I could have missed my flight?" I wanted to throttle him again.

We both stood and started an all-out run for the aircraft.

An explosion knocked us back into the mud.

The dread in my belly was familiar by that point in the war, but I knew I was in more trouble than usual.

It was a moonlit night. The explosion was like a beacon to all the Germans in the area.

The passengers!

I jerked up and started to run for the burning wreckage. I had to get the pilot and any passengers out.

Bullets hit the dirt at my feet and when one grazed my calf I knew I wouldn't make it to the wreckage. We were surrounded by German troops. Another glance at the wreckage and its resulting fireball told me there wasn't any "we" left to save.

I'd have to save myself.

I changed my course. I still had to run across some open field, but within a minute I could be back in the village streets. Then I'd at least stand a chance of finding a place to hide.

Shots rang out and I heard one whiz past my ear. The sound was like a hummingbird. I kept running.

But my hope for a hiding place was short-lived. I came upon a scene that ended all my hope for a long time.

People were being herded into the middle of the road and marched out of town. The Germans weren't in a good mood as they hurried them along.

I was dressed like any other local. I looked behind me, and saw the soldiers who'd been shooting at me gaining ground. I looked in front of me and saw a crowd I could blend into.

Die with one quick bullet or face unspeakable terrors in a death camp?

I turned toward my pursuers.

But then a vision flashed before me.

Esmée. Lille.

Esmée.

I ran into the crowd and threw off my jacket and sweater.

Within seconds I looked like anyone else who'd been hiding out for several years. In many ways I'd been hiding out, too. I'd just been able to move about.

I'd had a sort of macabre freedom.

In quiet tones I told the people around me that I would try to help them. I was Resistance. They all stared ahead, as if they didn't hear me. But they did, and unbeknownst to me at the time, I gave many of them hope that the liberation was closer than it was.

October 17, 1945

They marched us through miles of country-side. We were allowed to stop only after the first thirty hours. The older prisoners collapsed as we walked on.

I've never felt more helpless in my life. All they needed was warmth and nourishment, which may as well have been the Ark of the Covenant. Utterly unattainable.

It took us three days of walking, then two days on four different trains, crowded into cars worse than those in which you'd board your most expendable cattle.

How did I survive? By thinking of Esmée. Lille. Our life together after the war. I believed it would happen.

I needed it to be true.

Once at Bergen-Belsen—I now know that's what it's called—I was relieved to find out it wasn't the feared extermination camp, but it was a concentration camp nonetheless. Auschwitz survivors were there, as were prisoners from all over Europe.

As the Allies drove across Europe, the Germans moved their prisoners, still determined to follow through with Hitler's demonic vision.

No, there weren't gas chambers, nor row after row of firing squads.

There *was* typhoid.

At first it was hundreds, but by the time we were liberated it was thousands, who'd died from the fever. When prisoners got close to death, the order came down to give them a lethal injection.

I never had to do that. I can't say it would've bothered me as much as seeing someone suffer, as seeing the torture I did. But I didn't want to be any part of the Third Reich killing machine, and I never had to.

For this I am grateful.

I was put in charge of keeping the bodies stacked. As each person died, I was to remove the body from the camp bunker and place it outside onto the piles.

We didn't eat much. Some kind of soup that may once have been turnip soup, but tasted like cow piss. Of course, beef Wellington would have tasted like shoe leather in a place like that.

As I write this, it seems unreal. I still can't believe I'm here. So many didn't make it. I'd never conceived of such inhumanity before.

I existed among the death and suffering for a year and a month. I can't say I lived there, for that wasn't living.

From early March 1944 until our liberation in April 1945.

In April, the Brits came.

It was surreal to be liberated by my own countrymen. Once I trusted it was for real, and not another sick ruse to get us all together for target practice, I made my way to a British soldier. I told him my story.

"You're a Brit?"

"Yes, yes, I was SOE." No more need for disguises.

"Hey, Mel, there's one of us here!" he shouted to his colleague. It took a few days, but one night as I lay awake on that damned wooden bench a flashlight cut through.

"Jack Busher! Jack Busher!"

"I'm here!" By then I'd started having the fevers. I thought it ironic that I'd survive the war and this hell only to die of typhoid in the end.

"Bring him out, boys." The order was issued and I was lifted none too gently onto a makeshift stretcher. That night and for the next two days I was in isolation in an abandoned farmhouse they'd turned into a medical clinic.

As soon as they determined I could be transferred, I was on my slow journey back to England.

Reverend Tom and Pauline assured me it would be a relief to write this down. Get it off my chest, they said.

Horseshit.

It's scarred into my heart forever.

But my heart still beats, it still pumps my blood. And it still harbors hope that I'll find

Esmée and Lille safe and alive. And we'll all be together.

December 3, 1945

Esmée comes to me more and more in my dreams, and the horrors aren't visiting as often. The shock of that barbaric time doesn't fade, but if the nightmares are less frequent, I can start to think of living my life again.

Dare I dream of finding Esmée and Lille?

Will Esmée still have me?

Chapter 14

Nick walked into the old house and called out to Melinda's grandfather.

"Jack? Jack!" Usually Jack was out front in the mornings, and Nick found it odd that he hadn't run into him on his walk up the driveway, given the beautiful weather.

"In here."

Nicholas followed the raspy voice into the family room. Jack sat on his recliner, a natty blanket on his lap. If memory served him right, Esmée had knitted that afghan for Jack almost thirty years ago.

"Hey, what are you doing in here on such a great day?"

"It takes me a bit longer to get going nowadays. I'm

not a young man anymore, Nick." Jack reached for his cup of coffee and Nick noticed how shaky his hands were.

"Let me get that for you."

When Nick gave the mug to Jack, some of the coffee sloshed over the edge. Nick braced himself for the burn but it never came. The coffee was ice-cold.

"I'll go make us a new pot."

"Could you make it tea? That coffee's killing my stomach."

"No problem."

Nick walked back into the kitchen and rummaged through the cupboards to get what he needed. When Esmée was alive and well, the kitchen had been warm, inviting. She'd imbued a sense of quiet order through her home. Nick looked over at the large oak table that still had six chairs around it.

He'd courted Melinda at that table.

Shit.

Jack wasn't doing well, and Nick suspected it wasn't just grief or depression. The old man was a doer, someone who relished using his hands to build and create. If there wasn't gardening to be done, he'd be in his woodshop, working on yet another piece of furniture for another local church or store.

Those strong, creative hands had withered to half their size, and shook like the last autumn leaves.

Nick took him the tea and sat down in the chair next to his. Esmée's old chair.

"Here, let me." He held the mug to Jack's lips and noticed the sores around them. Jack sipped at the hot liquid and smiled.

"Thanks. I guess my age is getting to me today."

"It's not just age, is it, Jack?"

Jack sighed and drew the afghan closer to his neck.

"No. No, it's not just my age."

"Mind telling me what's wrong?"

"Yes, I do, but I will. That is, if you can promise you won't tell Melinda. Not yet. Not until she gets through the journals."

Again the journals.

"Fine. Tell me what's going on."

"After you tell me what's going on with *you*."

"Me?"

Nick slowly forced the air from his lungs, trying not to alarm Jack.

The old man didn't miss anything, however, even now.

"Yeah. I've been through war myself, you know. And it wasn't a cakewalk for me, either. I was wounded on the inside—my mind, my spirit—when I came back. I know a fellow wounded soldier when I see one."

Nick gazed into Jack's eyes.

"I walked by an IED at the wrong time. I'm not bitching, I'm lucky to be alive."

"Sure you are. But what happened?" Jack didn't miss a beat.

"I didn't lose what you're thinking of," he said wryly.

"I can still father your future grandchildren." If Melinda took him back. If they hadn't waited too long.

Jack laughed, and Nicholas was glad of the moment. The very secret he'd vowed to keep to himself until he got Melinda back was about to be shared with an eighty-seven-year-old World War II vet.

"That's good to hear. But what about your legs, the rest of you?"

"I lost my left leg. Knee down."

"Damn."

Jack was still as he took in the news. For a minute Nick was afraid he'd told the old man too much. Would this trigger too many memories, open wounds long buried under tough scar tissue?

"You walk fine. I thought you'd hurt your knee, sure, but I'd never have known."

"Rehab nowadays is impressive. Even though I'd do anything to replay that day, take another road, I've been very lucky. First, that they saved my other leg, and second, that they sent me to the best rehab in the country."

"In D.C.?"

"Yes."

"So you were there with Melinda?"

"I was there at the same time as Melinda. But I never contacted her. I didn't want to burden her."

And I wasn't going to beg her to come back.

"That's a tough break, Nick. But what about now? You have your old job back?"

"Yes, there's nothing wrong with me that'll affect my being an accountant."

"Do you still want to do that?"

Wise old man.

"I thought I'd do it until I can get a new business going." Nick took a swig of his tea. "I'd like to start a landscaping company here in western New York. Nothing too big, but the best-quality plants, shrubs and flowers. Throw in some custom-built wooden garden furniture and art."

"I didn't realize you liked to garden."

"I like it. I particularly like the idea of running a business, one that'll enrich people's lives." Nick stopped. He sounded like a dreamer. He'd have to make sure his spiel was more professional before he went to the bank for that small-business loan.

"What does Melinda think?"

"I haven't told her yet." Hell, he didn't know if Melinda was going to be in Buffalo a week from now.

"You two need to work it out, Nick. Esmée's told her the same thing, but Melinda's so afraid of rejection she'll keep going after what her father taught her was important, regardless of the personal repercussions. She's a family girl at heart, Nick, don't doubt it."

"So what about you?" Nick was eager to get off the subject of Melinda and him.

"What about me? I'm old, Nick."

"And?"

"We're all going to die sometime."

Nick swallowed his apprehension. He'd always appreciated Jack's candor over the years, but he'd also admired Jack's optimism. It was a quality he'd never had himself.

Isn't thinking you'll get Melinda back pretty optimistic?

Nick ignored his own thoughts.

"Yeah, but we don't die on our own time. I'm proof of that."

"You wanted to die out there?" Yeah, the old man missed nothing.

"Not at first. But there were some pretty low days, after the healing started. Even now I'll think my leg's still there and then…"

"Those dark times are dark, Nick. Some folks never have them in a lifetime, some of us have more than our share."

"You had yours during the war."

"Yes, and again when James was in Vietnam. He had his own dark days." And had handled them very differently from his father. Hid his trauma in drugs and booze until he sobered up twenty years ago.

As a kid, Melinda had never had the benefit of knowing her Dad. As an adult, she got along with him, and learned to respect him. But Jack had been Melinda's true father figure.

"So what's going on now?" Jack was still avoiding the issue.

"I have cancer."

"When did you find out?"

"A week after Esmée started chemo. I'd been tired and thought it was because of her diagnosis and then taking care of her. But our homecare provider encouraged me to go and get checked."

Jack shook his head and his face took on the saddest of expressions. "I've been through a war. I've been shot at, locked up, beat up. Hard to believe I survived all of that to die from this blasted disease." Jack didn't have to state the rest of his thoughts. Nick knew them.

The same damn disease that took Esmée.

"What kind of cancer?"

"Prostate. You know, they say most of us will get it if we live long enough."

"Yes, and that's why there are such good therapies for it." Nick's commanding officer in Afghanistan had survived a bout with prostate cancer and was very open with his troops about it.

"Not for me. I couldn't risk not being able to take care of Esmée."

Like a kick to the groin, Nick got it. Jack had given Esmée the last and final gift, after all.

He'd given her his life.

An uncomfortable twisting sensation gnawed at Nick's gut.

"Why not start the chemo now?"

"Too late. It's in my bones. Besides, I have no desire to artificially prolong my life. I saw what Esmée went through."

"It gave her a couple of extra years."

"True, but when the cancer came back, it did so like a devil and ruined her last few months."

Nick couldn't say anything. Hard to argue with a man who'd lived on the planet twice as long as he had and seen even more of death, horror, destruction. War.

"Melinda told me you were in a concentration camp."

"Yes. Bergen-Belsen is what they call it now. We just called it Hell."

"I'm sorry."

"Don't be sorry. Just make sure you always make choices that keep us from ever getting into a situation like that again."

Nick found himself unable to reply. Surely Jack had heard about the "ethnic cleansing" that was taking place all over the world. Did he feel his time in the concentration camp had been futile?

"Always tell your friends and your kids about it, Nick. When I came back, they didn't want us discussing it, and we didn't want to, either. It was too brutal, too inconceivable. We were all so glad the war was over, that's all we wanted to focus on."

Jack's hands fumbled with the edge of the afghan.

"When James came back, it was worse for him. At least when we went over to Europe, we were routing out a known, solid enemy. No question. But Vietnam wasn't just a war, it was an entire era everyone wanted to forget. James never got the recognition or support he needed."

"He doesn't blame that, or you, for his addictions."

"No, he doesn't. And those meetings he still goes to saved his life."

Nick looked Jack in the eye.

"It isn't always 'all's well that ends well,' is it?"

Jack sighed and let out a halfhearted laugh. "No, siree."

"When's the last time you saw the doctor?"

"Three weeks ago."

Right before he and Melinda got back. "And?"

"Like I said, Nick, it's in my bones. When I get too weak to be on my own, the same nurse who took care of Esmée can come and take care of me. They've offered me lots of drugs for the pain, but I don't want to be all fuzzy-headed."

Nick couldn't bear to think of this hero in any more pain. He'd suffered enough.

"Some of those drugs will keep you clear minded." Nick knew about painkillers first hand. He also understood Jack's desire for mental alertness.

Jack waved his hand in front of his face. "I'm sure I'll have to take them at some point. But not yet."

"Can I get you anything else, Jack?"

"No, no. Just don't tell Melinda about this. And wipe that wide-eyed look off your face, Nick. I'm okay, really. I'm just having a bad day. Tomorrow I may feel better than ever."

Nick doubted it but refrained from expressing his opinion.

He had to speed up his plan to get Melinda back.

After Jack died, she'd have no reason to remain in Buffalo.

Unless he gave her a reason.

Chapter 15

Esmée's Journal

May 13, 1945

Finally! A quiet moment. James is asleep and it's only nine. His earliest night yet since I started my job. I'm so lucky St. Mary's High School needed a French teacher. Because it's private, I didn't need a college degree, and the staff assured me they'd support me in my continuing education.

Of course, while the children are young, I can't think of going back to study. Maybe once they're in school.

I yearn for Jack—how nice to call him by his real name now that we're safe. I know it's beyond reason to believe he could have survived, but I do. I let the school's headmistress think I'm a war widow. I am, of a sort. I dream of a miraculous reunion.

Until then, I must provide for Lille and James. I am sorry to take advantage of the war to obtain employment, but this is America, the land of opportunity. The house I'm renting is one I may be able to purchase later, when my salary increases.

Maman's aunt Esther who sponsored me and the children is a dear and I visit her weekly. She's nearing ninety and it hasn't escaped me that a few more months and she might not have been in any position to bring us over. I am so grateful.

I haven't had the nerve to seek out Jack's relatives. They live two states away in Ohio, too far to drive easily. But I could write or phone… Perhaps one day I'll get my nerve up. I'm not ready to answer any questions yet. I'm not willing to give up my dream of Jack's survival.

Jack's Post-War Journal

January 3, 1946

Finally I can write without needing to stop because of the cramping of my calves or shoulders. The fevers are fewer and farther between. Still, the doctor and Pauline won't hear of me leaving to find Esmée yet.

Do they think she's just a figment of my imagination, dreamt up to get me through the hell I've lived through? Actually, I suspect they do. Fair enough. But they'll know the truth one day.

What I can't articulate to them is the guilt. I feel hopeless guilt that I survived. Why not the little boy I tried to warm in the dead of winter? Why did fever take him but it only tortures me?

Why couldn't I save the old woman who'd saved so many others in the camp? What about Gus, the man who assured with his last gasping breath that I'd survive?

No, I can't explain it to them. Esmée is the only one who'll understand. But I don't want to visit such horrors on her.

Esmée.

She's still alive, I feel it in my heart. And Lille. It would be so easy to slip away, take the ferry back to Belgium, find them.

But Esmée deserves better. She deserves a whole man. If I can ever go back to her—and I will—I have to be willing to let her go. She may be with someone else now.

Not if she felt the same as I do. But...maybe Pauline is right. Maybe I've made more of Esmée, of us, than is true. Could my ordeal have altered my memory that much?

No. Her creamy skin, her scent, they were real. Her heart, bigger than the earth, was real. Her cries of pleasure in my ear as I held her close and showed her my love were real.

Esmée is real.

Our love is real.

February 23, 1946

Each day grows longer. I feel the promise of spring and the hope that only an English summer can bring. Oh, Esmée, have you waited for me as I've waited for you?

I tried to call Belgium last week but no one answered at Esmée's home. I need to go there and find out in person what's happened to her and Lille.

Will she still have me?

The nightmares aren't as frequent, but they're still fierce when I have them. The constant agony, the blood. The battlefield is one thing, as it's an inhumanity with rules. But the concentration camp, it didn't have rules. As soon as I thought I'd figured them out, the guards would change them.

Bury one group of dead bodies, burn another. Save this child, let this other one die. Few children in the camp. The ones who made it there were destined to die of typhoid.

I couldn't let myself think of Esmée and Lille, lest I appear vulnerable. It seemed that vulnerability, any shred of human emotion, struck a chord with the guards. They were quickest to slaughter those who attempted any modicum of normal human decency. Better to behave like a robot with no feelings at all, better to complete only the next task assigned.

I didn't cry, I didn't rage. I stood and watched as body after body, arm after arm, foot after frost-bitten foot, smoldered in the death pyres.

I talked to Reverend Tom about this once or twice but even he doesn't want to hear all of it. He can only take so much. He never tells me to stop; he always stays and listens. Yet his body gets more rigid and his eyes look past me.

I long to hold Esmée and tell her how it our love brought me through my trials. That she doesn't have to worry about suffering anymore, either.

But what if she's met with harm? What if she didn't make it?

Melinda cursed the bright November sun. She'd prefer a dark gloomy day to match her mood.

Nick wasn't home, and just as well. She hadn't had the courage to ask him about his time in Afghanistan yet. Not in the detail she wanted.

She should start going through the house, deciding what she'd take to D.C. and what needed to be sold or donated.

There was no question that she'd sell her half of the house to Nicholas, but she wasn't going to saddle him with the extra feminine touches she'd added over the years.

Her heart, her soul, weren't up to the task. Truth be told, she didn't want to think about never coming back here.

Which was silly, since their divorce would be final by the end of next week.

She sank down onto the plush round area rug in what would've been their baby's room.

The baby that never came.

She knew of many women in D.C., friends and acquaintances, who got pregnant once they quit their high-stress jobs. Some had even adopted children, only to find that their body finally answered its own call to reproduce.

She sighed.

She couldn't base her life on anecdotes from other women who had men to go home to, men who supported their decisions to go back to work after the babies were born.

Nicholas had always thought she should stay home.

No, that wasn't exactly true. Nick just thought her job as a political aide was too demanding for a mom. That she might prefer exploring her creative side and doing something from home.

And she could always go back to teaching once the kids went to school.

But that had been *his* dream for her and their family. What about her dream?

She'd dreamt of having a family with no worries of her husband ever leaving. Her own father had been emotionally, as well as physically absent and she wouldn't accept that for her children.

Was that why she'd been so quick to jump at Nick's wartime deployments as personal affronts?

Jack's Post-War Journal

March 1, 1946

Am in a guestroom at the old farmhouse in Belgium. Belle slept at the foot of the bed. She remembered me. And made me miss Esmée all the more.

Esmée left the place to her sister. Even crippled, Elodie has survived the war and married! She and her husband, Nikolas, are expecting their first baby in the autumn. He and I swapped stories about the war and working for the Resistance. I have found a friend here who understands my struggles.

Took the ferry to Belgium yesterday in Pauline's old clunker of a car. Took six hours from Calais but I made it.

Elodie told me that Esmée packed up and left toward the end of the occupation and still sends them money. But Elodie didn't have a clue where Esmée was—she just had the postmarks from the letters, which indicated Buffalo, New York.

I shocked Elodie and her husband when I pulled

back the tapestry that still hung on that draughty wall. Pulled out two bricks and voilà! One of her journals, along with a letter for me, were intact.

Dear Esmée, she'd followed through with our plan. She's living close to my aunt Helen. I begged Elodie not to mention me to Esmée. I want to surprise her myself.

May 3, 1946

I'm back. We're back. Our family is united again.

I waited on the front stoop of Esmée's house— our house—for what seemed like an eternity yesterday. But it was only a couple of hours. I figured she'd be back from her teaching job around three or four o'clock, but she didn't show up until near five, her arms full of grocery bags as she pushed a stroller and Lille toddled next to her. My heart caught when I saw the second child in the stroller.

She'd found another man, had another baby? This quickly? She'd forgotten me?

But then I saw her face when she saw me. At first her expression was quizzical as she tilted her head, her dark waves spilling over her right shoulder. She wore a plain camel coat that ended at her knees. Her stocking-clad legs and high-heeled shoes were enough to heal my wounds, one by one, right then and there.

As she recognized me, her beautiful gray eyes

grew round with joy and excitement. The bags dropped out of her hands and she swept Lille into her arms and ran toward me.

"Jack!"

Her voice whispered into my shoulder as I stood and clutched her to me. We stood for a long, long time in that embrace. No kisses, just hanging on to each other as if we'd survived the *Titanic* sinking or an equally ominous disaster.

We had, after all.

She felt as I remembered her but better, if that's possible. Her hair caressed my face with its silky strands, and her scent was still Esmée. Only more sophisticated.

We would've stood there longer but Lille started to talk and tug at Esmée's dress.

"Mommy, Mommy."

"Yes, Lille." Reluctant as I was to let her go, I pulled my hands back to let Esmée kneel down next to me, next to Lille.

My daughter. Our daughter.

"Lille! Oh, Lille, guess who's home?"

"Who, Mommy?" Lille had her eyes on me the whole time. She was looking at me as though I were a murderer.

"Your daddy."

"Daddy?" Lille's intonation lightened and she giggled. "Daddy?"

"Yes, this is your daddy."

"Hello, young lady." She'd been a mere babe when I'd last seen her. Now she was walking, talking and full of her own cleverness. Heavens, I never could have imagined this delightful family. *My* family.

Lille didn't say much after that. She looked me up and down, then turned back to Esmée.

"I'm hungry. So is James."

James?

"Okay, love. Oh, dear, I've made a mess of the groceries, haven't I?" Esmée was at once endearing and shy as she scrambled to pick up the dropped bags. She threw cabbage, onions, bread and what was left of her eggs back into the sacks.

I took the opportunity to walk over to the stroller. Two eyes that were a familiar shade of violet-blue twinkled up at me, with lips curved in a baby smile. The baby in a blue flannel suit was smiling at me.

"Remember our last Christmas?" Esmée had walked beside me again, her voice soft and intimate.

I stared at her, then back at baby James.

"I named him James."

I had a son?

I had a son!

I whooped like a crazy fool as I lifted Esmée off the ground and spun her around the front lawn of the house I hadn't even seen inside.

"Esmée, is everything okay?"

A gray-haired bespectacled lady was standing in the driveway, holding a long umbrella, despite the bright sunny day.

"Oh, Mrs. Schaefer! I'm great. This is…is—"

"Her husband, Jack. Nice to meet you."

"Your husband? From the war?"

"Yes, yes!" Esmée actually jumped in her joy. I couldn't believe it. It was as though she'd been waiting as eagerly for this reunion as I had.

"Well, welcome back—we'll have a chance to get acquainted later, I'm sure." She turned her attention to my *wife*.

"Esmée, if you need any help with the children tonight, I'm available. They can spend some time at our place."

Esmée's face flamed. "No, no, that's so kind of you, but—"

"I won't let these kids out of my sight, you understand," I filled in for her.

"Of course!" Mrs. Schaefer nodded. "Well, just let me know if you need anything." She turned around and walked over to what was obviously her home, the house next to ours.

We went in and had the most wonderful dinner, the most wonderful evening with the children I think we'll ever have. It was like Christmas and our birthdays, only much deeper, much more significant. Reverend Tom and Pauline had warned me that it could be awkward or even difficult at first, but Esmée and I simply picked up where we'd left off.

We didn't speak of the war or our separation. There would be time enough for that.

After the kids went to sleep, I had Esmée to myself again. Alone.

"So you told everyone we're married?"

"Yes, well, they all assumed it, and for the children's sake, I wasn't about to correct them. They also assumed that you, that I, well…that I was a widow."

"I gathered as much. And you know, I wouldn't have you do this any other way. We *are* married, Esmée, and you are my wife. Forever."

"Forever." She said no more and instead showed me her feelings.

All night long.

I'd been afraid the war had left me weak, or unable to love a woman the way I wanted. But with Esmée, this wasn't an issue. At one point I was afraid I'd hurt her in my eagerness but she just laughed her rich husky laugh and wrapped her legs around my waist.

We were standing in the shower.

Esmée's Journal

May 28, 1946

Jack's been back for three weeks. It's been a dream. We wake for each other in the middle of the night, unable to satiate our need.

It seems like all we do is make love. At night and in the early hours before sunrise, yes, we do. Sometimes I don't even realize we're at it again until I look up into Jack's beautiful eyes and see his love for me. It's never died, even after all we've suffered.

After all *he* suffered. He didn't know if he'd live to see us again. And this is since the *end* of the war! Here I've made a comfortable home, dreaming of how he'd admire the curtains I've sewn, or exclaim in pleasure at the money I've been saving up from my teaching job.

Instead, he lay in the pits of hell, getting over the fevers and depression that came from the concentration camp.

Our priest married us quietly last night. I'd already confided in him when I first came here. He made it clear that if Jack ever did show up, we were to go see him immediately. I'm sure he's married many couples in similar situations since the war!

Jack is so enamored of Lille, and his surprise and awe at James made tears run down my cheeks with no regard to my rouge or lipstick. James is undoubtedly his son, and not just from the timing. I know, of course, that Jack is the only lover I've had since Henri, but Jack could have doubted me.

He didn't. James has his blue eyes and his square jaw. And when James toddles about the house he moves like Jack, stride for stride.

This must have been such a shock for Jack. He

thought he was coming home to Lille and me, and now he has a son, too. A lesser man might have recoiled, or even left. There are lots of these stories. How the war has changed everyone and how many couples struggle. But Jack and I fit back together as though we've never been apart. As though we'd had years together before our separation, and not the few days we actually shared.

Yet there's a huge part of himself he's keeping from me.

I feel it when his gaze wanders outside to the fruit trees, and I know he's not seeing the beauty of our garden or our home, but some haunted memory. His whole body tenses and he looks as though at any minute he'll jump behind one of those trees.

"Jack, what's wrong?"

"Nothing, Esmée. I'm just a bit tired. I think I'll take a nap."

He disappears into the garage, where he's setting up a woodshop, or upstairs to our room, and doesn't talk for hours on end. My friends at school tell me it's not unusual and he'll get better with time. Sometimes I wonder.

There's a position at the State University of New York for a professor of English literature. Jack used to teach before the war and his credentials are outstanding. I don't think he'll have any problem getting the job. But I do wonder if he'll be able to manage the schedule of teaching and the commute every day. He can take the bus at first, but within a few months we should have enough saved to buy a car. He'll have to get used to driving on the right side of the road!

His new salary will help us achieve our goal of eventually moving out to the suburbs and buying our own home.

Melinda placed Grammy's journal in the acid-free, archival-quality carton she'd purchased at the local art-and-crafts store.

Even Grammy and Grandpa Jack suffered through his Post-traumatic Stress Disorder, as it was called today. But it didn't sound as though they had the resources offered to modern troops.

The container she'd chosen for Grammy's journal made her reflect that today's scrapbooking was a way to preserve a life's story, just as Esmée's journal did.

She ran her hand over the box. The whole scrapbooking craze had never hit her, as she preferred to read or go for a walk in her precious spare time. But she had several friends who boasted about how caught up they were on the scrapbook pages that reflected their lives.

But if she did make her own scrapbook, what would it look like?

The earlier years would be full of hopeful greens,

blues, yellows. The beginning of her marriage to Nick would be framed in flowers and she'd have a page dedicated solely to their garden, with a gazebo in the center.

The last two years would be a white background with black text—or maybe the other way around. No smiling photos.

Melinda fitted the cardboard top on the carton and blinked back tears. Had her life been *that* bad these past two years?

Yes.

"I have a wonderful career that challenges me, I have friends and I'm not stuck in Buffalo." She spoke to the empty room.

But you're stuck in your own misery.

"Great." Now her darkest fears were talking to her as she talked to herself. What next—she'd start seeing messages in her teacup?

And truth be told, the idea of being "stuck" in Buffalo didn't make sense to her anymore. She felt comfortable here.

As though she'd finally come home.

Chapter 16

The kitchen door opened with a blast of air and banged against the doorstop that prevented the knob from punching through the rose-print wallpaper.

Melinda jumped out of the reading chair.

"Great day out there, isn't it?" Nick smiled at her as he shut the door behind him with his foot.

That door always gave her a jolt when it slammed.

"What, did I surprise you?"

Melinda remained quiet. Her professional demeanor fled at the first sign of Nick. Would he consider her a traitor if he knew she'd spent this entire Friday at the library, researching him?

She looked down at her hands. The chipped French

manicure and grown-out acrylics seemed to smirk up at her.

"Yes. No. I mean, I thought you were working today."

Nick shrugged out of his coat.

"You know the great thing about surviving a war, Mel?"

"Ah, no."

"It's given me a chance to focus on what's important. And working on Lederman's books for the rest of the afternoon just isn't that important today."

Lederman was the local funeral home and one of Nick's clients.

"Oh, no?"

She didn't know what was more difficult. Standing up straight and trying to appear nonchalant while this gorgeous man spoke to her as though she were his sole interest in life, or simply letting go of the bitterness between them long enough to enjoy a real conversation.

"Are you okay?" Nick threw his jacket over a kitchen chair. He leaned on the counter. He used his cane less and less but still relied on support from the counters and walls. "You look kind of peaked."

"I'm fine. I just need something to eat." She made her way over to the kitchen and pulled a can of soup out of the pantry.

"Want some?"

"No, thanks. I ate with Jack."

"You were at Grandpa Jack's?"

The sharp stab in her stomach wasn't from hunger. Why did Nicholas think he could just go over to Grandpa Jack's without talking to her about it first?

Why do you think it's any of your business what he does?

"Yeah. I like to stop in and shoot the breeze with him now and then. He's got to be lonely up there on his own."

"I know." Melinda squelched her guilt. Why had she let an eighty-seven-year-old man tell her where to stay? Strong-willed Grandpa Jack or not, she needed to be more solicitous, more insistent on looking after him.

"He understands that you're reading the journals and doesn't expect to see you until you're finished."

"I know." She dumped the soup into a pot and added the requisite can of cold water.

"You can stop torturing yourself, Mel."

The proximity of his voice was her only warning before his hands were on her shoulders. She fought the urge to lean back into his strength.

"I know."

"If you know so much, why do I get the feeling you feel responsible for your grandparents?"

Melinda stirred the soup. She'd missed his touch. So much.

"I wasn't here for her or for Grandpa Jack."

"You knew when you left that there were no guarantees, Mel. We all did." She didn't comment on his admission that his leaving wasn't the perfect situation, either.

"Has it occurred to you that your brother, David,

hasn't even been out here once in the last five years, save for Esmée's funeral this past summer?"

Melinda didn't like the fact that Nick was comparing her role to that of her much younger half brother's. Even if he *was* a grown adult who could help Grandpa Jack.

"He's not the child they raised. I am." Besides, Aunt Lille had been here to help.

"What are you learning from the journals?"

She stared at the stove's backsplash as she stirred her soup, willing the liquid to heat up more slowly than normal. Nick's massaging of her shoulders and neck were pure bliss.

"That I've only ever known a small part of my grandparents' lives. I had no idea what they'd sacrificed for me, for my father and aunt. I don't think I'd have the strength to do what they did."

"It's all relative. Each generation does its part."

"Yeah, well, we haven't had to go through an occupation by the enemy, nor have we lived in a concentration camp."

She heard the harshness of her words too late. The warmth of Nick's hands disappeared and she felt the void where he'd stood.

"No, but there are other horrible things...."

She turned around.

"I'm sorry, Nick. I haven't been through what you have. It must have been so hard over there. But you never talk to me about it. *Ever.*"

"I prefer to leave it back there, in Afghanistan. But

maybe we would've fared better if I *had* talked to you more."

His admission stunned her as much as it obviously stressed him. She saw the lines etched around his eyes, his generous mouth. Instead of revealing his fun-loving nature they told the story of his suffering.

"Did you lose many friends, Nick?" She stepped over to him and placed her hand on his arm.

"Yes." He stared at her hand for a minute before he covered it with his own. The he lifted it to his lips and kissed the tip of her index finger. As he spoke, he brought her hand to his heart. Melinda felt his heartbeat through his flannel shirt and closed her eyes. God, he smelled so good.

The scent of pine, the outdoors, Nick himself.

"Melinda." She opened her eyes and looked into his. "Yes, I lost friends. But the greatest price I paid was losing you. Us."

"Nick—"

"Don't say anything right now, Mel. Despite your statements otherwise, I know you've missed me. And that I still get to you."

"That's pretty arrogant, isn't it?" She yanked her hand out of his.

The narrowing of his eyes should have warned her.

"What kind of soup are you heating up, Mel?"

"What?"

Maybe the war had affected him in ways she couldn't see, like in his brain.

"Tell me. No, don't look at the can." He grabbed her shoulders. Not in a threatening manner, but with enough force to stop her from finding the answer.

"What kind of soup are you making, Mel?"

"I…I don't know."

"Take a look."

She walked to the stove, where the soup bubbled in the old pot.

She looked at the empty can on the counter. *Spicy Diced Tomatoes.*

Not soup.

"Spicy tomato."

Nick's rich laughter rolled around her. She hadn't opened a can of soup. She'd reached for a can of spicy stewed tomatoes and hadn't even noticed.

"Aw, honey, it's okay. Just proves you're as human as the rest of us."

Melinda dumped the mixture down the drain and flicked on the disposal.

"I'm human, all right."

She wished she could shove her tears down the disposal as easily as the chopped tomatoes.

Nick knew a good time to leave when he saw it. Melinda would only rebuff any attempts he made to comfort her. He'd done enough damage already.

Whenever he thought he'd gotten another inch closer to her, the real Melinda, something like this happened. He only ended up distressing her.

"I'll be in the shed."

He pulled his coat back on and headed out to his one remaining refuge—his workshed. He and Jack had spent hours working together, either here or in Jack's shed. He turned on the light in the refurbished metal hut and felt his rapid heartbeat slow.

He inhaled the aroma of all the different woods he'd used over the years.

The cold air surrounded him and felt damper than the sun-washed air outside, so he turned on the space heater near his feet. His leg needed the warmth.

His latest project stared him in the face. He'd gone over to Jack's to coax the old man to help him with it. Before he knew how sick Jack was.

Maybe Jack would have some better days before the cancer won out, but Nick wasn't so sure.

The fine grain of the cherrywood glistened in the afternoon light. He hadn't varnished it yet, but it was such fine wood he could all but see the gleam of the finished work.

Cherrywood—Melinda's favorite. And the one thing she'd always wanted during their marriage but he'd been unable to make for her. He hadn't had the time or the inclination.

He sighed as he trailed his fingers along the grain of the rocking chair.

He'd wasted so many weekends at football or hockey games, leaving his new wife home to fend for herself. If he'd just taken the time to grow up and devoted a few of those hours to their relationship, would things be different today?

He rubbed his hands over the unfinished piece. The corner had a rough spot that caught his palm. A box of sandpaper sat next to the chair and he grabbed a piece of his finer grain. As he rubbed the wood, he prayed he could breathe the same life into his failed marriage.

Chapter 17

Esmée's Journal

June 8, 1947

Haven't written much these past months as one day seems to blend into the next. The kids are getting so much more active and they keep me busy when I'm not at school.

Jack's temperament worries me. It was all so wonderful—almost too perfect—after he returned last year. Starting around Christmas, though, he'd wake up drenched in his own sweat after moaning through another godforsaken nightmare.

He has these fits of temper over the stupidest things. Yesterday he threw his pruning shears across the garden when a rose thorn stabbed his finger.

I don't have any fear that he'd ever hurt me or the children, not intentionally. But his temper is bewildering. I worry about him but he won't discuss any of this. Just tells me we're finally getting used to being around each other every day.

I'm not so sure.

July 15, 1947

Now I have a name for Jack's problem. Our family doctor, whom I spoke to in the strictest of confidence, told me it's *combat fatigue*. They used to call it *shell shock* in the Great War. I remember that now. Maman and Papa would talk about their parents and relatives who'd returned from the trenches in such a state.

But I always thought it was more pronounced, not this subtle erosion of the man I love into a cranky, brooding fellow.

Dr. Simuliewsky assured me that he'll recover. It may even take a few years—God, I hope not!— but as long as I continue to provide Jack with a loving home and a regular routine, this, too, shall pass.

September 6, 1950

Anyone who reads this will be bored as so much of it is drivel. Sad to think that my daily life amounts to what's in these pages. I used to have such hope when I wrote. Today I don't.

I went to Jack's office finally, at the university.

I suspected the worst and found proof.

My validation began last week when I asked him why he'd been late for dinner twice in three days.

"What, don't you think I have enough pressure on me without you questioning my work, too, Esmée?" He rubbed his temples, loosened his tie. His skin reflected the heat of Indian summer.

"I don't question your work, Jack. I question your whereabouts."

"So you've traded teaching French for private investigating?"

He shook his head and poured himself a generous helping of brandy. He never used to drink except occasionally wine at dinner.

"Why do you force me to ask you, Jack? It's not as though you can't pick up the phone and call me when you're going to be late."

"So now I have two bosses."

His sneer said all I needed to know. Somehow, over the past year, he's come to despise me. He views me as his jailer, his keeper—not as the partner I was so certain I was.

"Jack, it doesn't have to be this difficult." I walked over to him and tried to put my arms around him. He shrugged me off.

"No, it doesn't. But you keep making it that way." He topped off his glass. "I'm going to the back porch to read. Call me when dinner's ready."

That night I entertained thoughts of putting a laxative in his portion of meatloaf. Of course I didn't.

Yesterday I decided that whatever, whoever, is distracting him at work, I deserve to know about it. When he didn't show up for dinner at five, I asked Tami Jenkins, the next-door teenager, to come over and babysit Lille and James.

I changed out of my teaching clothes and wore my sexiest back-zip black skirt. New lace-topped stockings, pumps and a snug acrylic sweater completed my outfit.

Dressed to do whatever it took to get my husband back.

It was after hours and the department receptionist wasn't in her usual swivel chair in front of the entryway. I was relieved, as she could have stalled me if she wanted to protect Jack.

I headed back to his office and saw the light spilling from beneath the old door and through the frosted-glass window that bore Jack's name. JACK BUSHER Associate Professor. If he managed to get tenure as he expected, they'd have to change the sign to PROFESSOR JACK BUSHER. I know tenure's been on Jack's mind of late. But he doesn't make it any easier with his disconnected approach to our family life. Even the kids notice his distraction.

I considered knocking first. I should have, should have spared myself the pain. At some level I knew what was going on before I opened that door, before I walked over to the university. A woman knows when her lover is straying, even if it's just in his mind, just a glance at an attractive stranger.

I knew.

But still I opened the door with a quick turn of the porcelain handle.

I heard them before I saw them.

The hollow giggle of the young student, her perky breasts straining through her tight blouse as she leaned in to Jack. His silly response to her laughter, a low grumble as he wrapped his arms around her waist. His hands, the hands that had caressed me while we made James, while we both healed from the war, clutched at her impossibly small waist.

"At least you're both still dressed. Commendable."

If I hadn't been so distraught with betrayal choking my every breath, I might have laughed at their too-quick response. The girl jumped out of Jack's arms and he sat up straight in his desk chair, eyes locked on mine.

"Esmée—this isn't what it looks like. We're…

we're studying a piece of literature and got to a funny part."

"Yes, it's a little-known Shakespearean sonnet." The girl's voice was a little too breathless.

"Which one? 'Taming of the Horny Professor and his Slutty Pupil?'"

"Esmée." Jack's voice actually held a tinge of recrimination. As if *I* was the one without manners.

"Did you tell her I've killed for you before, Jack?" Jack's eyes widened and I thought he might faint.

The girl scampered for the door. I wasn't done with her. I grabbed her upper arm and resisted my urge to shake her until her pearly teeth fell out.

"Here's a newsflash your mother obviously didn't teach you—married men are always a dead end. It might be a great romp, but it's always a dead end. Because a married man always has a woman like me at home."

I did my best imitation of an evil witch with that last line. The girl shook under my hand, but she still had the gumption to twist away from my grasp and run out of the office, her cheap heels clacking down the corridor.

"Dammit, Esmée, was that really necessary?"

I turned all of my seething self back to him. The man I had loved, nursed back to health, prayed over, missed for months on end.

My husband.

"It was more than necessary, Jack," I said calmly. "And you know what else is necessary? For you to get your sorry ass back home and spend the rest of your days making this up to me and to the children."

"It's not that simple, Esmée."

"No part of our life together has been simple, Jack. But that's no excuse to piss it all away for a collegiate fling. You're too old for this."

I turned around and walked out. I didn't say anything else to him or I'm afraid I might have started blubbering, and I couldn't do that.

I wouldn't.

If I smoked, I'd be halfway through a pack by now. But I don't smoke. I don't even drink enough to ease this pain. I think I sounded bold and confident but it doesn't take away the hurt I'm carrying inside.

Melinda wanted to stop reading. Lie to Grandpa Jack and tell him she'd read it all, or that the pages were too faded to discern. This was the definitive TMI—too much information.'

Grandpa Jack had cheated on Grandma? Well, if the student was still dressed, as was Grandpa Jack, then it sounded like nothing had happened.

Nothing irreparable, at least.

Yeah, right. How would *she* feel if she walked in on

Nicholas in similar circumstances? She'd told herself over the past two years that she had no problem with Nicholas seeing another woman. They were through.

So why did she identify so closely with Grammy's pain?

Chapter 18

"We need some heavy leaf bags." Melinda perused the list she'd made before they left the house.

"And another rake." Nicholas limped along the endless aisle of autumn-related tools in the huge home-improvement store. Obviously his leg injury was aggravated by the damp weather and the time he'd spent in the shed.

Melinda blinked away sudden hot tears as it occurred to her that if the clock was rolled back just a few years, this would've been a very happy day for them.

Another Sunday together.

But today hadn't started with slow, easy lovemaking, nor had she come up with a cozy meal to enjoy in front of the fire tonight, watching a new DVD.

She'd had to get out of the house, away from the journals. Nicholas was on his way out and she'd asked if she could join him.

She watched him study the assortment of rakes standing in various containers along the aisle.

"Looks like they've been picked over." She eyed his hands. His strong fingers grasped one rake and tested it for weight.

"Yeah, but we need one of these. I've got the whole back half of the yard to go, and it's too damp for the leaf blower to handle."

"I should've come home last month." She made the observation but didn't realize she'd spoken aloud until Nicholas leveled a sharp look at her.

"And done all of this yourself? No. Your timing is perfect."

"Are you being sarcastic?"

"Not at all. That's just how it is—things have a way of working out the way they're supposed to."

"You're not just talking about the leaves."

"No, I suppose not." He placed an aluminum rake in their cart. He seemed to lean on the push handle more than necessary.

"Your leg bothering you?" She tried to keep her tone light. He'd never admit anything to her if he sensed concern or what he interpreted as pity.

"This cold damp doesn't do it any good." He started walking, his limp barely noticeable as he pushed the cart toward the lightbulbs.

"Would you rather use your cane?" She nodded to where he'd put it in the cart when they first entered the store.

"Nope, this is fine."

Then why are you gritting your teeth?

She sighed. He hadn't opened up about what had happened to his leg, but the pain etched across his face told her enough.

Several minutes later, they stood in the inevitable long line for the cash register. As soon as they'd checked out and were back in the warm car, Nick turned to her. He smiled, not a regular smile, but the one he used to get what he wanted.

It'd almost always worked on her.

"Why don't we go have some fun after this?" His eyes sparked with an excitement she recognized, although she hadn't seen it in months. Years.

"Fun?"

"Yeah. I've been doing too much work, and you've had your nose stuck in those journals for hours. Let's go play."

They played for the rest of the afternoon. First stop was the cider mill. The mixture of freshly crushed apples and concord grapes created a pungent aroma that threw Melinda back to grade school.

Children crowded around to get a glimpse of the processing equipment that poured the liquid into waiting plastic jugs. Nick bought them a jug of each, and Melinda picked out two caramel apples to have in the car.

"Don't eat yours yet—let's go have a picnic," he said.

Nicholas was in fine form, what Melinda used to call his "date mode." He had the radio on full blast as they drove through the sun-speckled day. No conversation was necessary.

She decided to just let go of their past and enjoy the moment. She felt the weight lift from her chest—she hadn't realized how much energy it took to protect her heart from Nick.

I can allow myself this one day.

After an hour of highway driving, Nick pulled into the most beautiful piece of land in all of western New York.

Letchworth State Park.

A month earlier, they could have reveled in the spectacular colors of the leaves. By now most had fallen, but the bare limbs backlit by the azure sky cast their own spell.

Nick wound the Jeep through the park, away from any picnic areas or gazebos.

Melinda knew where he was going and didn't even try to resist.

The "Grand Canyon of the East" had been part of their shared history, from their early dates to their wedding fifteen years ago. They'd chosen Letchworth for their honeymoon. A cabin, the woods and their love, for five uninterrupted days in the fall of her twenty-fifth year.

"We were different people the last time we came here," she murmured.

He glanced at her from the driver's seat. "We were different each time we came up here, Mel."

But we were still "us."

She left the thought unspoken.

He stopped at the grove of small cabins and killed the engine. The moment hung in suspension between them. The pull of his gaze forced her to turn toward him.

"Nick—"

"We can still leave, Mel. I just have to turn the engine back on and we're out of here."

His eyes reflected years of knowing her as each one of her staccato breaths punctuated her longing.

"Not yet."

Her quiet consent was apparently all he needed.

Nick pulled her to him so fast that his kiss swallowed the rest of her breath. Melinda held on to his shoulders with clenched hands, her head back, her mouth open to Nick's tongue and whispers of endearment.

"I've missed you so much," he groaned against her cheek. His teeth found her earlobe while his hands unwrapped her scarf and started to unbutton her coat.

She marveled in the sheer sensuality of his caresses. His lips felt soft and insistent at the same time. His kisses ignited a need she'd ignored for too long.

She wanted him *now*. In the car, in the woods, wherever.

Her body trembled for him and her heart cried out to him.

She shut down her thoughts. No more recriminations, no bitterness. Just these hours with Nick.

He was fondling her breasts, and her breath caught when his fingers lingered intentionally on her nipples, taut through her cashmere sweater.

"Nick, don't stop."

Her hands were shaking but her mind was on one purpose—to get his shirt up and his pants off. She reached for his belt buckle with one hand and for him with the other. His erection filled her hand and his gasp reverberated through the car.

"Oh, baby, no. Wait a minute."

His hands grasped her wrists, then he drew her hands to his chest.

"Wait. One. Minute." His eyes remained closed, his mouth open. He appeared in need of oxygen as much as she. She looked at the steamed-up windows. Proof positive that they'd been about to complete the deal.

"Nick? What's going on?"

He sat all the way up and turned the key in the ignition so he could lower the windows enough to clear them.

Still throbbing with need, Melinda's body was taking longer to switch gears.

What now?

"Melinda, I haven't been totally honest with you." Nick stared through the car's windshield, out into the spectacular view of the gorge.

He could've been studying the deer that meandered down what looked like a sheer cliff.

But Melinda knew better.

Knew *him* better.

He was trying to figure out the best way to tell her something.

Oh, God, please don't let there be someone else for him. Not another woman.

The thought pulsed through Melinda. Any mental cobwebs their lovemaking hadn't swept away were now sandblasted into oblivion.

"Nick, we're both adults. There's no reason to keep things from me."

She fiddled with the toggle on her hood's drawstring.

"But you don't have to…to tell me all your secrets, either," she added.

Couldn't she say *anything* smoothly?

"This isn't a secret, but it's going to be a shock for you. It has been for me."

His mouth was set in a grim line and Melinda saw the struggle in his eyes. Whatever he was about to say held great importance for him. He looked as though he was poised on some kind of brink—the gap between what reality was for them now, in this moment, and what it would be once he told her…whatever it was.

"Tell me, Nick. Just spit it out."

"I lost my leg in the war."

"Your leg—"

"It was an IED. I'm lucky to be alive—"

"But I was never called—"

His hands were warm as they covered hers. Shudders

raced across her back, and her own hands trembled with the force of her shock. Nick held them tightly.

"Stay with me, Melinda. Breathe."

She nodded, her eyes closed. She was trying to live through the moment. Overwhelming nausea made her skin break into a clammy sweat.

"I'm sorry, Nick." She wrenched her hands out of his and opened the car door.

She found the nearest clump of trees and threw up.

Several minutes later, resolving never to drink so much fresh apple cider on an empty stomach again, she felt his hands on her shoulders.

Nick sat on a boulder beside her. For a man with one leg he sure moved fast. He half pulled, half dragged her onto the boulder with him.

"Melinda, I'm so sorry. I should've told you sooner."

"Damned right you should have! You could've been killed!" Her rage startled her, but she didn't back down from it. She couldn't. Not anymore.

"But I wasn't killed. I'm here, and I can lead a normal life."

"Where did they send you after…after it happened? *When* did it happen?"

"I was initially at Landstuhl in Germany, then they sent me to D.C."

He moved toward her. Looking at his thighs, covered by his worn jeans, she couldn't tell which leg it'd been.

Only because of the cane did she know it was his left leg.

"It happened in May."

"What day?"

"The fifteenth."

Their anniversary.

"You were in D.C.—afterward?"

"Yes. We were there together."

But *not* together.

Melinda leaned her head on his shoulder and focused again on her breathing.

"Mel, I wish I could say I didn't call because I didn't want to hurt you or worry you. But we were so mad at each other at that point and—"

"I hadn't been there for you before you left."

"No, you weren't." His voice was quiet, acknowledging without judging.

"I'm so sorry, Nick."

"So am I. But that's behind us now, isn't it?"

Melinda wanted it to be. But she couldn't bring herself to mouth the words.

"I'm lucky because I can still drive an automatic, no problem. I still have my arms and hands, so I'm not too limited in my activities."

His expression was somber, frank.

"I saw many more folks in far worse shape than me. I just had a clean loss of limb."

"I wondered why you didn't let me get too close. But I never thought the cane and your limp meant you'd lost a leg!"

"You wouldn't unless you saw me undress or shower."

The reminder that they hadn't shared such an intimacy in over a year left Melinda speechless.

Silence ticked by.

Nick wondered if he'd shared too much too soon. But it couldn't go on like this. Their attraction had started to get the best of them, and he didn't want Melinda to find out he was missing part of a leg when they were in the middle of making love.

But she'd never been one for casual sex and he didn't think that had changed.

He'd had to tell her.

Now it was up to Melinda. Would she have him back?

"I'm just glad you're alive, Nick. That you survived."

Her face was drawn, and sweat still glistened on her throat, her cheekbones. Her eyes were still closed, her head against the bench.

"I read about this a few days ago," she said. "On the Internet."

"You never said anything. You knew it was me?"

"I put two and two together." She took a deep breath. "So who was the soldier who died?"

"My friend Tommy. He wasn't from western New York. He'd been put in our unit as a fill-in. He has three kids and a wife. Widow, I mean."

"You went through hell, Nick."

"I did. But you don't look so hot yourself right now. What are you thinking, Mel?"

She waved her hand feebly in front of her face.

"It's been a shock, that's all."

"That's all?" He tried not to be so obvious in his disappointment.

She took in a deep breath. He found his gaze riveted on the rise and fall of her chest.

His thoughts remained on his one desire—to win her back and make love to her like he'd never made love to her before. He'd had enough time during night watches on the ground, and then in rehab, to think up all the ways he could make her moan.

"Are you trying to make me feel worse, Nick? I've already told you I should've been there for you. I should've been available to you before, during and after both of your deployments. But I wasn't. So now you tell me you lost your leg. How am I supposed to reconcile that with my horrendous treatment of you?"

"Melinda, you—"

"Don't, Nick." She held up her hands. "We both know I was useless to you. So now I'll have to live with that for the rest of my life. Where were *your* thoughts when you got blown up, Nick? Were you distracted by your hatred for me, or by your hurt that I wasn't there for you?"

She buried her face in her hands, then raked her fingers through her hair.

"The worst of it, Nick, is that each day for the rest of your life you'll have a constant reminder of this. Of our broken marriage, our failure to be there for each other. My failure to you."

Her gaze met his dead-on. Nick no longer saw the girl he'd married or even the young woman he'd left behind.

In her eyes was a wisdom he'd ignored this past week and a half.

"It's a two-way deal with us, Melinda. I wasn't the best husband for you. I could've been more understanding of *your* needs. Your desire to be challenged professionally."

"Maybe. But I didn't have to go so far away to be challenged. I was running."

"From me."

"No, not from you, Nick. From what we'd become— hell, what we *didn't* become. From what I saw as a failure to have kids, a failure to grow together, to communicate. From who I'd become."

"Don't be so hard on yourself."

It was as though she hadn't heard him.

"You know, Nick, I've been reading Grammy and Grandpa Jack's journals, and they're more than just words or a history lesson. They show what we all go through, how we can all make choices."

She was speaking more quickly, her words coming out more smoothly than they had a few minutes ago.

"By running away I didn't make a choice. I opted for the easy way out of a tough situation." She leaned toward him, almost touching him.

This was getting better.

"I didn't want to look at you, to love you and know I could lose you at any moment. I didn't want that to be part of our reality."

"It hurts too much." He understood.

"Yes."

"They told us in the field that it's common to have a big fight with your wife before you leave. It's easier to get a kick-in-the-ass out the door than to say 'I love you with all my heart, goodbye.'"

Her eyes shimmered in the morning light.

"They were right." Melinda looked down and he saw her stare at his legs.

"Why didn't I figure it out sooner?" she muttered.

"There's no reason you should have. It's cold out, I'm wearing jeans or pants all the time. My feet are in regular shoes. I've hardly got a limp anymore."

"Does it hurt?"

"Not so much now."

"I saw a documentary on television about IEDs and amputees. Do you still feel as if the limb's there?"

"Yeah. But I know it isn't."

"Where, uh, how much—"

"Jack asked the same thing."

Her eyes widened.

"Yes, I told him last week." He sent her what he hoped was a reassuring smile.

"I lost my leg just below the knee. The knee that's left isn't as mobile as it once was, but it still bends fine. My prosthesis is great. I'll show you the details sometime if you're interested. And no, my, uh, privates weren't involved, except for a few pieces of shrapnel."

"Shrapnel?"

"The size of slivers. Caused lots of swelling but didn't affect my swimmers."

"Dammit, Nick! You almost died and you're talking about your *sperm?*"

She gave him the look that conveyed her belief that she was married to a perpetual fourteen-year-old.

He gave her his best "and don't you love it" grin.

Melinda relented, and her stern face relaxed in a smile.

Score one for the offense.

Chapter 19

Esmée's Journal

December 17, 1954

It's crazy of me to even think I could've carried a baby to term. I'm already thirty-two, and I've had my child. James was so big, and the midwife told me then that I'd best not try to have another after all the blood loss. She said something about my womb being "lazy."

But I still hoped. When the doctor told us we were pregnant, he cautioned me, but still I hoped. I hoped against hope that this baby, this pregnancy, would prove them all wrong.

I made it to almost five months. She made it to almost five months.

She was a little girl, our little girl. I named her Rose. We buried her in the church cemetery. I knew nowhere else to put her. Jack came undone at the sight of the tiny casket. I just worried about whether she'd be warm enough.

Is this my punishment for what I've done in my life? For what I haven't done? For failing to love my first husband? Was I supposed to stick it out? Is this the price for Lille and James? For Jack?

Jack won't talk. He's locked in his own pain. We just got through all his postwar troubles, and our life looked so good.

I felt so good. The baby was kicking and Jack laughed each time he felt her under my skin. He'd missed this with James; now was his chance to enjoy the whole experience with me.

For us to make a baby together. The whole process.

But no, it wasn't our time at all. Just more hell. I was so sure I'd seen hell, lived through it. I had no idea, did I? This is hell. This is the darkness that won't go away. The night of my life.

What do I tell Lille and James?

Melinda stared at the single entry from 1954. Just this one. No wonder.

Poor Grammy.

She'd suffered so much during the war, and now this?

Melinda didn't know what it was like to be pregnant, or to suffer a miscarriage, but she knew what it was like not to be able to have a child.

She flipped through the next pages. All were either blank or had entries from 1955 and 1956. Nothing more was mentioned about the baby, Rose. It was as though those dark times had never existed.

Did Grammy think of Rose every day, and keep her child in her heart? Melinda knew about Rose—Aunt Lille had said Grammy lost a baby when Lille was in middle school.

Aunt Lille also spoke about a time when Grammy was "dreamier than usual."

Melinda supposed that, back then, before the advent of antidepressants, Grammy must have been given tranquilizers.

If she'd ever even taken them.

After reading what Grammy and Grandpa Jack had gone through, she didn't feel she had any more room for self-pity or even self-loathing. Her life was what it was, and she'd created this mess with little or no help from Nick.

But she was going to need his help to undo the biggest mistake she'd ever made. Would he be willing to help her now, after she'd been such a blatantly fair-weather wife?

* * *

Nicholas walked in to a changed home. It had looked the same from the outside, except for the curl of smoke that wisped out of the white-bricked chimney. The shutters needed scraping and painting—he made a mental note that with the spring thaw he'd get them done. No doubt the gutters should be cleaned out, too.

He breathed in the aroma of some wonderfully seasoned meat.

"Melinda?"

Maybe Melinda had been kidnapped and replaced by the Melinda he used to know. Maybe this was some kind of freak reality show, like "Almost-ex-wife Swap."

He heard her footsteps a moment before he saw her descend the stairs. She wore opaque black tights and a short wool skirt that emphasized her Rockette-quality legs. His gaze took in her black cashmere sweater with the deep V that elicited a reaction in him that would surely set off the fire alarm if such things could be physically measured.

Other than by his body.

"Hi, Nick. How was your day?"

Damn. She *had* been swapped.

"Great. But it looks like my evening might be even better. Unless you're expecting someone else?"

Crap. Too late, he realized that to assume all of this was for him was not only foolhardy, it was stupid.

"No, just you. I thought I'd make dinner since you've finished your first week back at work. You deserve to celebrate." Her expression faltered. "Unless you, um, have other plans?"

"No, none at all." He hung up his coat in the closet and drew in a deep breath. Did this mean that Melinda might want to—

"Would you like some wine, beer, soda?"

"Just a soda for now." He didn't need the waves of relaxation from a glass of Merlot adding any impetus to his hopeful imagination.

He hadn't imagined their growing emotional intimacy since their afternoon at Letchworth Park on Sunday, but he didn't want to push her into making love with him.

Not yet.

"Here you go." Melinda was lightning-quick, as though she'd been ready to serve him whatever he wanted on the spot. He looked at this new woman in front of him.

"Did you get your hair cut?"

"What?" She wrapped a strand around her index finger. "Oh, yeah, I stopped in at the salon and had a trim. Why, is it too short?"

"No, it's very sexy, actually." He watched her eyes widen, her pupils dilating as she took in his compliment.

"Oh."

What he really wanted to say was that her new cut reminded him of how her hair looked after he'd made love to her, all rumpled and disheveled from the activity.

But he thought she probably knew that. Wasn't that what these purposefully messed-up dos were about?

"What else did you do today?" He sat down in his favorite leather recliner. He couldn't keep standing or he'd be tempted to grab her.

"I read a lot more of the journal."

She sat on the couch in the corner nearest him and curled her legs under her skirt. Nick forced his eyes away from the space that winked out from under her skirt. He'd never finish their conversation at this rate.

"Any new revelations?" He longed to share his own revelation of Jack's selflessness but was sworn to secrecy.

"Yes. Too many." She bit her lower lip and took a deep, shaky breath. It was the way Melinda always looked when she was fighting back tears.

"Like?"

"Like Grandpa Jack fooled around on Grammy when he was a college professor."

"No kidding? That doesn't sound like him."

"That's just it. It *wasn't* him. He was a shell of himself, because he didn't have a healthy way to deal with the war."

"But what about his journal? You said his doctor and minister told him to write it."

"Yes, and while he was writing it, things were going well for them. But there aren't any journal entries from Grandpa Jack during any of this time. He drops off a few years after he's home and doesn't pick up again until Aunt Lille and my dad are grown up."

"What does he write then?"

"I haven't gotten that far. But I can tell there are entries from Grammy for that whole time. I need to finish reading them."

"This is getting to you, Mel. Maybe you should tell Jack you're through and leave it for a while."

"No, I can't. I promised, and it's for Grammy, too." Her voice drifted off and he saw her swipe at a stray tear. Then she squared her shoulders. "I have no business being sad. We live such an easy life and we have so much. Are you more aware of that since you've been back?"

Her question sucker punched him.

"Yes, yes, I am."

More than you know. A whole leg's worth, a whole marriage's worth.

"Give me an example, Nick."

She wasn't going to let him off easy.

"Well, I appreciate being able to walk, for starters. I value that this is a neighborhood we can walk in. It's a good place. I can walk to work, to the coffee shop, to the hardware store. What could be better?"

He hoped his lighter tone would encourage Melinda to lighten up, too. This was too close for comfort. Maybe he should've taken her up on the beer.

"Those are practical things. But what about *you*, Nick, your heart, your moods, your surviving a war? Aren't you glad you weren't in a camp like Grandpa Jack?"

"Sure, sure I am." He sucked down so much soda that the bubbles ran up his nose. He coughed.

"Are you okay?"

"I'm fine. When's dinner going to be ready?"

"Soon." She kept staring at him with a look he couldn't decipher. Wonder, sadness, pity?

No, not pity. Melinda hadn't made one move to help him with anything, any more than she had before he'd told her about his leg. Which was just the way he wanted it.

"Go ahead, ask me whatever it is that's pinging in your brain, sweetheart."

She smiled.

"I'm grateful for a lot, too, you know."

"Are you?"

"Yes." She got up from the couch. "But I have to go get dinner now. We can finish this later."

He watched her move in the short black skirt. He'd always loved that look on her.

And she knew it.

Esmée's Journal

August 22, 1962

Both of my babes are gone. Lille has stayed here in western New York but we decided to pay for her to have a room in a large student house. She has a nice-sized room and the bathroom's next door, shared with five other girls. Lille is determined to become the next Madame Curie.

It's a big change from the free-spirited teenage girl we'd learned to live with while she was in high school. I'm laughing as I write this because it's past, and Lille's a model college student now, but these past four or five years with her have been hell at times. I thought I'd lose my mind. But she settled down and has apparently listened to something Jack or I have told her over the years.

I hope the best for her, but I know what young love can do. If she happens to meet her soulmate she may change her mind about academics. She's also expressed interest in traveling through Europe, even trying to find out if any of her biological family survived the war.

James went back to California yesterday. He's growing his hair too long for my liking, but he's a young man now, away from my apron strings.

We were fortunate to have a great week at the lake and enjoyed a clambake on the beach Friday night.

"James, why don't you have some food with your beer?" Lille never stopped poking fun at her brother.

"When I need the advice of a nerd, I'll find you, I promise."

He tilted the bottle of Labatt's and took a long swig.

"James, Lille is right. College life isn't all just beer and girls."

"Yeah," he told me. "There're lots of other leisure activities to indulge in."

His tone bordered on insolent, just past smart aleck. "James!" Jack's voice cut through the night air. The cool breeze already had us in hooded windbreaker jackets, but I felt only heat when I looked at my husband.

He was fighting mad.

"Aw, Pop, chill." James didn't read body language the way I did.

"As soon as you do." The threat in Jack's voice alerted my senses. Before I could think of anything to defuse the altercation, Jack strode over to James and yanked him up by the collar.

"Jack!"

"Dad!" Lille's strident shriek followed my plea. "Don't do it, Dad. It's just the beer talking."

"Yeah, man, what she said." James glanced at his father with sheepish eyes. "I was just fooling around."

"Get over there." He pointed at me. "And apologize to your mother." James looked three years old, caught with his hand in the front parlor candy dish.

Jack relaxed his hold on his son's collar and slowly stepped back. His hands were no longer on James but his gaze never left James's face. "No more funny stuff, young man." Jack's voice vibrated with his displeasure.

"Yes, sir," James muttered under his breath. He shuffled through the sand over to me.

"Sorry, Mom."

"Okay, honey." I went back to my clams. I honestly didn't know what to say to him anymore. My boy had turned into a young man in a blink, and in the transformation he'd left behind all his manners and common sense.

"You're too easy on him, Esmée." The aluminum chair frame squeaked as Jack sat down next to me and placed a large paper plate full of steaming clams on his lap.

Fortunately the kids were eating on their own, at a table several yards away.

"I'm not being easy, Jack. I just don't know what to do with him. You're better at dealing with him at this age."

"You speak as though he's still a child and going through another developmental phase, like learning to tie his shoes or use the toilet."

I sighed.

"Honey, I want to enjoy our last night with both of our children, our family. Can we save this for later?"

I felt equally concerned about James. These were tough times to raise children. But for one night I just wanted to be with my family. All of us, for whoever we were. No more, no less.

Jack grunted. After a while he got his usual good humor back and we traded stories about when the children were younger. James and Lille gravitated toward us and sat in the sand nearby, holding their plates.

"So you brought us both from Belgium and moved straight here?" James asked.

"Yes, that's right." I knew Jack didn't want any elaboration. The kids had never asked whether or not we'd all been together when we first came over. They just assumed we were, and Jack and I left it at that.

"Actually, it took me a bit longer to get here." Jack mentioned it as casually as if he were talking about his vegetable garden.

"Why?" Now Lille's interest was piqued.

"I had business to finish after the war."

"What kind of business?" James sounded skeptical.

"War business."

We all let the statement lay. I watched light from the bonfire play across Jack's face but didn't see any regret or pain. Just resignation.

Maybe he's finally let go of the demons that have haunted him.

"After we clean up, I thought we'd have one more dip." I'd worn my bathing suit under my jacket. Lake Erie was warmer than the air this time of year.

"Sure, Mom." Both kids kept eating. I stood up and brushed my fingers on my napkin.

"Want to go in, Jack?"

His eyes reflected the same mischievousness I'd first noticed more than twenty years ago.

"Beat you." He was a blur of jacket, pants and shoes as he stripped down to his swim trunks. He was waiting for me by the time I swam out to the buoy.

"No fair!"

"Ah, Esmée. Come to Papa."

I laughed as he pulled me closer. The buoyancy of our bodies made for wonderful friction in the water. He found my bikini bottoms quickly enough and my laughter turned to gasps.

It wasn't a one-way game as I made him gasp, too.

April 11, 1967

James came back today. It's been two years since we've seen him. He acted himself, yet more mature, even apologetic for the way he left home six years ago.

Jack and I never understood his need to "find himself." When we were young, there wasn't time for that. Of course, if I think back far enough I suppose I had his attitude when I was fourteen, maybe fifteen. But the war put an end to any future self-seeking. To us it merely seems indulgent.

But James wanted to go to Berkeley, so we

supported him. What should've taken four years has taken him nearly seven. We last saw him when he came home his freshman year for the holidays. He wasn't in the house much even then.

The difference is that now he's "found" himself, he wants to change the world. He's involved in many political activities. He's assured me they're all patriotic and for the best.

Jack didn't react the way I thought he would to James's return. He's happy to see his son but still disappointed that James didn't have more direction earlier in life. Blames himself, I suppose. When James needed Jack as a boy, Jack was suffering from his blue moods, up until James was five or six.

But they've long since passed, and the man James once knew as his father has been replaced with a thoughtful, kind, loving man. A man who took up arms and fought for his country, for the cause.

James made it clear a while back that he was against the war in Vietnam. No surprise for a student at Berkeley. But his attitude about it is different now. It's not that he supports war but he seems to think he may have a role over there. He saw some of his classmates go over, including his roommate. He and Earl were good friends from the start.

He told us Earl was killed last month. It's hit

him hard. He believes he could've made a difference if he'd been with Earl.

We've lost a few young boys from here but no one James knew well.

May 28, 1967

Should've seen this one coming. After spending time with his father, James has realized that perhaps Jack is a better role model than he thought. That his father might just know a few things about life, after all.

James seems determined to stay off whatever drugs he tried in California; he won't even drink a beer with his father. But they sit out there on the stoop and talk about all kinds of things.

So when James got picked for the draft he only stood silently as he read the notice, then turned to Jack and me.

"I'm going in the army. Next month."

"Oh, James." I couldn't say anything else. This was his response? This was the same young man who'd claimed he'd go to Canada if he got drafted?

My gut reaction was to grab him and throw him in our car and drive him the forty-five minutes to the Canadian border myself.

Of course, I didn't.

So James leaves in a month. We have our son for one more month and then I have to let him go again.

June 15, 1967

My pen is shaky— No, *I'm* shaky. I'm a grandmother.

Not the way I planned.

James showed up with Melinda today. His four-month-old daughter by that hippie girlfriend from Berkeley. Turns out he wasn't sure she was pregnant when he left California, but she was. So here we are, with a granddaughter he needs guardians for. His girlfriend Peacock Feather—what kind of name is that when she's obviously of Irish-American descent; James says her name used to be Penny Higgins—has taken off. Abandoned her own daughter.

Tomorrow we'll see to the paperwork at our lawyer's. We'll have exclusive custody of Melinda until James returns, which should be in fifteen months. He has basic training, then he'll be commissioned an officer due to his college degree. He'll pull a one-year tour of duty and receive his thirty days' leave.

Melinda won't remember him when he gets back.

Why this common theme through my life? Why am I once again raising a child?

Another little girl.

But not alone this time. I have Jack, and we have Lille to help us.

Lille has excelled at her studies at the state university in Buffalo. She works in the lab every day, far into the evening. She'll soon have her Ph.D. in cancer research.

But even she needs a break and she takes it on the weekend. Lille adores playing auntie to Melinda, and Melinda has taken a shine to her. Good thing, since Melinda is motherless.

Melinda shook her head. She knew her biological origins. She knew that "Peacock Feather" was found dead just six months after she'd abandoned Melinda, leaving her with James in Buffalo. From heroin. She'd learned that her mother had been an orphan; perhaps that was the source of her pain, the pain that had triggered her addiction.

Had her mother done heroin when she was pregnant?

But Grammy had never mentioned anything unusual, and Melinda had never experienced anything in the way of ill health that could be attributed to a drug-addicted mother.

Melinda admitted to herself that she hadn't tried very hard to get pregnant. Her infertility was more likely of her own doing. Sure, she'd talked about it, but

Nick hadn't been that excited about leaving her pregnant when he knew he was going off to war.

Yet Melinda wondered if her baby issues had more to do with her fear of becoming a mother like own....

It was time to ask some questions, and there was one person she trusted to give her a straight answer.

Chapter 20

"I was wondering when you'd show up." Aunt Lille's voice had lost none of its charm over the years.

Neither had Aunt Lille herself. She embraced Melinda in a heartwarming hug and held on for a few minutes.

Just long enough to make Melinda feel guilty about not contacting her aunt since Grammy's funeral.

"I know you're busy with your new grandbabies, Aunt Lille. I'm glad you're home and not working today."

Melinda allowed herself one more moment of Aunt Lille's embrace before she pulled away. Eyes gray as newly shined pewter twinkled beneath shaped black eyebrows. Aunt Lille's hair must've gone gray years ago but she'd always kept it colored and styled.

"And I'm so sorry I waited until today, the day before Thanksgiving, to come and see you," she added.

"Renée and Desirée will be here tomorrow, you know."

"I can't wait to see Desirée's baby!"

Melinda and her twin cousins had been more like sisters when they were growing up. Three years apart, they'd attended the same elementary and high schools, and Renée had gone to the same college as Melinda.

They'd been best friends and confidantes.

Melinda and Renée saw each other often when Melinda was in D.C., as Renée worked at a research lab in Bethesda, Maryland. But she hadn't seen Desirée, who lived in Boston, since her baby shower in September.

"I've missed everyone, but I only have two weeks and with so much to do…" She let her voice trail off.

Maybe she should be having this conversation with her father, but he was ensconced in Arizona with her stepmother, Jillian. In any case, she'd chosen someone who'd been far more stable in her life.

Aunt Lille.

"Dad said he gave you the journals."

"You know about them?"

Aunt Lille laughed. "Honey, I read them years ago. Your grandmother wanted me to understand where I came from." She shook her head nostalgically.

"I read the journals up in the attic—in my private space."

Both Melinda and Lille laughed. Compared to

James, Aunt Lille had always been the more adventurous child when she was younger. Always exploring, pushing the limits. James had been a straight arrow—until he went away to college.

Lille, on the other hand, had grayed Esmée's hair prematurely with her constant motion and inquisitive nature. When Melinda was growing up at Grammy and Grandpa Jack's, Lille had mellowed into a studious graduate student intent on finding a cure for cancer.

"How did *you* react to the journals?"

Aunt Lille thought a bit before she answered.

"I was enthralled by them. I was amazed that my mother, the French teacher at St. Bernadette's, had survived the German occupation. I was equally astounded by how she met my dad, and how they both rescued me from what would've been, well, certain death."

Aunt Lille's eyes narrowed, as though she saw a definite point in space that depicted her parents' nightmare.

"I suppose those journals are why I chose the career I did. I wanted to cure something, as though that could wipe out a fraction of what my parents suffered. *All* my parents."

Melinda glanced at the crystal Star of David Lille kept on a shelf, prominently displayed. She seemed to draw comfort from this symbol of her biological parents' faith.

Aunt Lille wore a tiered purple velvet skirt and

cashmere lilac twin set, the image incongruous with this woman so keenly attuned to humanity's suffering.

Melinda had visited Aunt Lille's lab at the university campus and knew the hours she spent, first at a lab counter and now in front of a computer, decoding the genetic causes of cancer.

She'd received her tenure as a professor years before her contemporaries, for no reason other than her brilliance and dedication to her task.

"Did the journals influence you to choose someone like Uncle Jaro for your husband?"

Melinda often thought that Jaroslav Ravas displayed many of the same characteristics as her grandfather. Strong, silent and full of emotion once you got past his exterior.

A Czech, Uncle Jaro had immigrated to the States when it was nearly impossible for any Eastern Bloc citizen to travel, much less defect. He'd walked through the mountains in 1968, and as a writer, he'd used his connections with Western journalists to get to the U.S.

"Yes, and of course, his great ass." Aunt Lille revealed her dimples with her smile. "I don't believe we completely control who we choose as our mate."

"The 'nice ass' factor." Melinda smiled back at Aunt Lille.

"Speaking of ass, what's going on with you and Nick, Mel?" Aunt Lille was astute in all facets of life, and had been able to read Melinda's moods since Melinda was a child.

"I don't know. I mean, I *did* know, ten days ago." She ran her fingers through her hair and realized she hadn't even combed it today.

"So, what happened?"

"He served me with divorce papers five months ago. I thought it was over."

"And now?"

"And now we're cooped up in that little house and he's being so understanding, so real." She fingered the hem of her skirt. "He's still as aloof as ever, though."

"Tell me more about being cooped up in the house."

"I didn't even know he was back. He came the night I arrived. He's due to start work right after I leave, although he's been working on and off."

"And he made it through the war okay, except for his leg?"

"How do you know about his leg?"

"Dad told me."

"Oh." Everyone in her family knew more about her husband than she did.

"Aunt Lille, do you think he could have what Grandpa Jack did, after World War II?"

"It's possible. Just as your dad turned to the bottle after Vietnam. Of course nowadays we talk more about things like post-traumatic stress disorder, PTSD. But isn't he talking to a professional? I imagine now that he's back here in his civilian environment, it's quite an adjustment from the day-to-day routine of the military."

"And war." Melinda bit her lip. "No, I don't think he's seeing a counselor. Maybe I'll suggest it."

"Or not. He may be content just to share it with you. It may be all he needs."

Aunt Lille stood up and turned toward her gourmet kitchen. Melinda had missed spending time with her. The hours baking together, the long talks over hot chocolate, coffee or wine, depending on the occasion.

"Listen, Mel, I've got some imported tea I just bought. Would you like to try Manic Mango or Stop-Your-Flashes Cohosh?"

"Manic Mango sounds great."

Melinda followed Aunt Lille into the copper-accented kitchen. The island that dominated the room was topped with black granite and surrounded by high wrought-iron stools. Melinda slid onto one of them and leaned on her elbows.

"I always feel so at home here, Aunt Lille." She glanced at the refrigerator magnets that were loaded down with candid shots of her cousins' kids.

"Thank you, dear. It always feels more like home when you're here." Aunt Lille measured some herbal tea leaves into a red ceramic teapot and pulled two matching mugs off their copper hooks over the sink.

"So what are you finding in the journals that's making you rethink your marriage?"

Always to the point, Aunt Lille.

"I'm thinking I've been so selfish, so self-centered about my career and Nick's military assignments. I really have behaved as though the whole world revolved around me, haven't I?"

"Don't be so hard on yourself. He wasn't always emotionally available to you, dear. It was natural for you to seek another outlet for validation."

"Yes, but I ended up leaving him in his hour of need. I mean, most wives support their spouses when they deploy. Instead I got mad and left for D.C.!"

"For a job that was a lifelong dream. Why not? Why shouldn't you have?"

"Because I should've been here for Nick. Given us another shot."

"It doesn't seem too late for that now, Melinda."

"But now the senator depends on me."

"No offense, dear, but every job is expendable, no matter how important and socially significant it might be. Especially compared to making a marriage work, raising children."

Aunt Lille caught Melinda's expression and stopped her reply with the wave of one hand.

"No, don't go into that right now. You can always adopt. My point is that nothing's more important than family and you chose Nick as your immediate family years ago, just as he chose you."

"But now he's unchosen me."

"Let me tell you something. Last week I got to hold my new grandbaby, Michela. She was wriggling around and making her three-week-old presence known to all. As I held and watched her, I knew without a doubt that if I had to give up everything I've accomplished professionally just to hold her once, I'd do it."

Aunt Lille rummaged in a drawer for a potholder.

"I've been given other talents and been blessed to utilize them to help others. But my most important accomplishment is my family. Period. End of story."

Aunt Lille removed the whistling teakettle from the stovetop and poured the water into the pot.

"Wow."

What could Melinda say to top that? Aunt Lille had twenty-four years, two kids and three grandchildren on her. Melinda had never felt so young and immature in her life.

"It's something we all have to figure out, Melinda, but I've learned that I'd kill for my family. Without them, I have nothing."

"Speaking of families, I was wondering if you knew any details or facts about my mother's drug use when she was pregnant with me. Is it possible I can't have children because of it?"

Aunt Lille paused for thought. "All your check-ups, exams, they're normal?"

"Yes."

"And Nick's?"

"Yes."

"Well, then, my dear, I'd say you have nothing to worry about there. Except—don't wait. At your age, your hormones can shift overnight and lessen your odds. Get moving!"

Letter from James

December 15, 1968

Dear Mom and Dad,

I have no idea how much of this letter will reach you. I'm told the staffers black out whatever's classified. I can't tell you where I am but I will tell you it's hotter than hell and the mosquitoes are bigger than the hummingbirds in Dad's flowers.

Already one month since I left Basic. It's a bit difficult to be in charge of all these young guys. Most of them are straight out of high school. I'm not like those Academy grads, and I think they like the fact that I'm more relaxed. But what they don't realize is that if I were an Academy asshole— sorry, Mom—I'd have at least half an idea of what I'm doing.

My goal each day is to keep us alive, safe for the night. Our nights are the busiest.

I can't thank you enough for taking care of Melinda. How is she? Is she walking yet? Hell, I don't know what a baby does when. I wish you could've known Penny—Peacock Feather—before the drugs got to her. You'd know she was very artistic and loving. She enjoyed, and graduated with honors in my class. She was all set to go to graduate school but got into the war protest instead. Unfortunately she got into drugs, too.

I'm scared Melinda doesn't have a mother but

*she's got you, Mom. Have you been showing her
how to knit? Are you teaching her French?*

*I will write again as soon as I'm able. I miss
you both and let's hope Nixon does what he says
he will and gets us out of here ASAP.*
Love,
Jimmy

The letter had been tucked into Grammy's journal.
Melinda knew her grandparents always referred to her
father as James, yet he signed his correspondence with
Jimmy. She'd ask him about it the next time she saw
him. He'd probably have a lot to say about the journals,
and about his years in Vietnam. But she suspected he
wouldn't have wanted to talk about it.

The only other reference to her father's experience
in Vietnam was an official document from the U.S.
Army informing Jack and Esmée that their son, James,
was MIA. Missing In Action.

Another, shorter letter was attached to it, stating that
James was now considered a POW. Prisoner of War.

Both were dated January 1969.

Melinda remembered her last visit to Arizona before
Grammy died. She'd sat in a Starbucks with Dad and
Jillian, and they'd touched on the highlights of their
lives together. A life that had started when Melinda
was six and her father married Jillian.

The adjustment when he got back from the POW
camp was wretched. Melinda remembered begging her

grandparents, "Please don't send me away. This is my home. This is home. With you."

They were only walking her five doors down the street to her dad's place. But it was a different world to her. A world where she had to show her dad how to take care of a little girl.

Dad didn't respond to her every need. No, he had to be told. In exact terms.

But later Melinda knew it had been good for her, too. At her grandparents' she was the center of the universe and that often transferred to school, to the classroom. When Melinda didn't get what she wanted she'd simply tell the teacher "My grandparents will take care of this."

And sadly, she'd believed it.

Even sadder, it *was* true.

James, though, weakened by his war experiences, wasn't willing to put up with such spoiled behavior. He wanted to give Melinda a good basis for her life and he didn't feel that catering to her every whim was the way to do it.

But a recent POW survivor, especially after Vietnam, wasn't emotionally equipped or cognizant of the myriad needs of a little girl. Melinda continued to spend much of her time at Esmée and Jack's.

Jillian, too, was a lifesaver.

Her quiet, patient nature helped nurture James back to health, and her understanding of children enabled Melinda to make the transition from her grandparents' home. Jillian became more than a mother to Melinda; she was her friend.

But the bond between Esmée and Melinda had been forged in blood and could never be broken. Jillian saw that and never got between Esmée and Melinda. She understood their closeness and knew Esmée would protect Melinda with her life if need be.

And then Jillian got pregnant with David, ten years Melinda's junior. Most of the attention shifted to him, to the son her father had always longed for.

On the threshold of adolescence, Melinda took the fawning over David as affirmation that she wasn't adored by her father, but Jillian helped smooth her tumultuous feelings. And the fact was, Melinda had adored her baby brother.

The last time she'd sat and talked with her father and Jillian was when they were all in Buffalo after Grammy's funeral. She'd met them at a coffee shop before they flew back to Arizona. During that visit James told Melinda he wished things had been different for her, but he would never regret that she'd had the opportunity to know her grandparents.

"Had I been in the picture more, you might not have become as close to them." He sighed. "I was a hardheaded pain in the ass in my youth and put my parents through the mill. At that age, I would've interpreted their every offer of help as an attempt to control me or my family."

"Problem is, I didn't feel I *had* a family, except for you." He stared into his coffee, and Jillian kept massaging his back in the little circles Melinda swore must have worn dents in her father's spine.

"You had Grandpa Jack and Grammy, too. You just didn't realize it."

Jillian nodded her approval at Melinda over James's back.

"Besides, all's well that ends well, right? It all worked out. I had Grammy and Grandpa Jack, *and* I had the two of you. You had a chance to get to know your parents again, in a different way."

"Yeah. I'll never forget how proud the old man was when we brought David home."

Melinda couldn't stop the twinge of envy in her belly. She loved her brother and had loved him as a baby, too. But he'd received the attention her father hadn't been able to give her.

And *he'd* always had his mother.

She knew her resentment hurt only her, but it still sat there, a lump of discomfort she hoped she'd one day get rid of.

Somehow.

"Remember how Grandpa Jack helped you with driving-instructor duty when David turned sixteen?"

Jillian laughed. "Esmée gave me a good stiff drink when all three of them took the new Mustang convertible for a spin."

"She did?" Esmée had enjoyed a glass of wine with her meals like any good European, but Melinda had never seen her imbibe in anything other than wine with dinner.

"Yup. A martini." Jillian smiled at the memory.

"Was it good?" Melinda had sampled her share of cocktails at D.C. social events and enjoyed many of them.

"Horrible. The worst sort of cough medicine imaginable." Jillian chuckled. "But I was able to gag it down. After all, once I'd taken two sips, the rest was no problem."

During that conversation Melinda had thought that her dad and Jillian's view of their shared past was somewhat skewed but she didn't mention it.

All's well that ends well, she told herself. As always, Shakespeare said it best.

Chapter 21

Esmée's Journal

October 17, 1985

It's quiet in the house today. Jack's out back working on the bulbs. Every October I wonder what possesses him to go out there in the most windy, rainy weather. But come April and May, when the garden is shouting with color, I'm so glad he did.

Had James over for dinner yesterday. Jillian is a dear, and I'm glad he found her. For all our sakes. They're talking about moving to Arizona. Melinda's very busy in school, getting ready to go away to college next year. We don't get to see her as often anymore. I think it's almost a month since our last chat.

So many changes! Can't believe it. My baby girl, growing up. Lille says it'll be harder on me to see her go than it was to see Lille leave for school. In some ways she's correct. Because with Lille and James, it was a matter of survival for so long, that there was no chance to indulge them. The five years I was raising her and James and also working while Jack struggled with his "spells" all blend together in my mind.

When I read back in this journal, I see that each day held its value, its gifts, but whole months, years, blend together in my memory.

I had Melinda all to myself for quite a while. Sure, Jack was here, but he was still working and couldn't take off as much time to be with her. I could take a sabbatical when needed.

James looks so much like Jack at his age. But Jack was more gaunt, more haunted in his demeanor. I imagine James had an awful time as a POW but he never discusses it. Just like Jack...

September 5, 2002

Good morning! God, if You'd ever told me I'd be alive to write this, I wouldn't have believed it. I'm eighty years old today. I feel more like, I don't know, fifty. Maybe even younger. Yet my skin's wrinkled and my bones ache on cold days.

But I still have my overall health, my peace of mind.

And Jack.

It's been Jack all along. Even before I knew him, my heart did. That's what made that horrendous time with Henri bearable, no matter how excruciating it was. I was convinced something better was waiting for me, but I didn't know how to get to it.

Then You dropped Jack into my life. And Lille, James. Melinda, Desirée and Renée.

Lille has planned a party for me. Just a quiet dinner, she says, but I have a feeling she and the girls have been brewing up something a little bigger. We'll see.

My granddaughters continue to provide me with the greatest joy. Lille's girls, Desirée and Renée, have stayed closed to their mama, even though I swear, one day they'll win the Nobel Peace Prize. They work under Lille at the university and one day will be credited with the big cure for cancer, I'll bet. As twins as beautiful as they are, they could be fashion models but never even considered it. Just stuck to their studies like their mama.

And Melinda. My oldest granddaughter. From the time James brought her over until today, she's been a constant light in my life.

I do worry about her, though. She and Nick have tried to make a baby, with no luck, and I'm afraid she's letting that pressure get to her. Of course, I don't know how hard they're really trying. I do hope she's not expecting a baby to solve whatever is or isn't going on in her marriage.

In the old days, we'd just hope we were pregnant. It seemed easier back then.

Except during the war.

I don't think about the war as much anymore. It was so long ago. Now the kids are all worried about terrorism. I don't think we've ever been safe, truly. But it's so important to live our lives to the fullest each day, and not let the bad guys get us down.

I remember trying to remain strong and optimistic when the Germans occupied Belgium. There were days I wanted to stay in bed, under the covers. Never go out to the bakery or walk down that street again, where the Nazi officer often stopped me.

I could've been killed so many times. If he'd found out I was Resistance. If Henri had found out. If my neighbors ever thought I'd anything to do with the Nazi officer.

I think of my high-school acquaintances who lost their lives either during the war or right afterward. Some even became traitors and supported the Germans. I don't believe I could ever have been a traitor, but why were they drawn into the enemy's web?

Why was I spared discovery—and death?

Silly old girl, I am. It wasn't because I was as

headstrong as Melinda is today. I had memories of how things had been before the war. I had a vision for how it could be again, and I was determined not to allow anyone or anything to interfere with that.

Even an occupying army.

I'm wearing the pink silk suit I bought when Jack and I went to Toronto last year. We saw *Mama Mia* and had the best Indian curry. Thank you, God, that my stomach hasn't gone the way of so many, unable to enjoy any flavor. My friend at the senior community center, Anne Marie, only eats rice, potatoes and fish. What's with that? I need my flavor.

I hear Jack getting ready. He's still so handsome after all these years. My eyes see the old man he is, and the mirror tells me I'm an old woman. But in my heart we're young and full of the promise of life.

The hard years are finally memories.

Esmée's entry ended abruptly. Melinda looked ahead and saw that the next entry wasn't until a year ago, right around the time of her ovarian cancer diagnosis.

Melinda remembered Grammy's eighty-fourth birthday all too well.

She and Nick had made love that Saturday morning, and it was as enjoyable as ever. But once they were in the bathroom taking showers and getting ready, their companionship went sour.

"My unit's going to Afghanistan again." Nick kept shaving as he spoke, as if he'd just told her they needed more toilet paper.

Unconcerned, Melinda kept applying her mascara. Last month, Nick had agreed to leave the Reserves.

"That's no surprise. We knew it would redeploy more frequently since 9/11."

"I'm going with them, Melinda."

She paused midswipe, the mascara wand in front of her eye.

"Don't be silly. They can't make you. You resigned your commission."

"No, I never did."

A punch in her gut.

"What?"

Another break in their communication. There'd been a lot of them lately. But none as serious as his going off to war for the second time.

Leaving her alone.

"You thought I should resign, Melinda. *You* thought it was time for me to get out of the Reserves. You want one less tie to bind us to western New York, since you've decided you want to move to D.C. I never agreed to anything. You just assumed."

Melinda felt like one of her old stuffed animals. Full of holes, with her insides hanging out.

"I can't believe you didn't tell me!"

"Tell you?" Nick's lip curled with the derision she now realized had been there long before today. His eyes sparked with anger and something else she didn't want to see.

Disgust?

"You haven't wanted to discuss anything with me if it didn't involve your ovaries or your job. It's all about you, Melinda. You getting pregnant, you finding the right career path. But there's someone else in this marriage, babe. Me."

She stared at him. What was that ancient story about scales falling from one's eyes? She'd just experienced it. For the man she saw before her bore no resemblance to the man she'd married fourteen years ago.

This Nick was still handsome, strikingly so, but fiercer, more determined. His curly golden locks had been replaced by short, silver-sprinkled hair that accentuated his smoldering eyes.

But he had a hardness, an edge she'd ignored. And that edge was painful when she bumped up against it.

"I don't have anything to say to you." She'd turned and left the bathroom.

They'd avoided each other for the entire party.

When Grandpa Jack presented Grammy with a beautiful diamond-encrusted World War II aircraft pendant, Melinda had snuck a look at Nick. He stood stock still, his expression flat.

No sentiment for him.

Melinda remembered swallowing gulps of bitterness and resentment with each sip of champagne.

At the time, it'd been the end of her trust in Nick as

far as she was concerned. But from her current stand-point, she saw that perhaps she'd been incredibly selfish. Just as selfish as he'd implied.

Chapter 22

Thanksgiving 2007

Melinda took her time in the shower. It was Thanksgiving morning, and they planned to spend the day at Aunt Lille's with her family and Grandpa Jack.

Maybe she and Nick could have a shot at it, after all. Maybe, just maybe, they could give their marriage a second chance.

She brushed her hair until it shone and took special care with her lotion. She had good reason to—Nick might be touching her again.

Everywhere.

And she him. Was she up to it? Was he?

He'd lost a leg. She knew she needed to come to terms with his status as an amputee, but right now she still had trouble dealing with the knowledge that he'd almost been killed. She'd almost lost him.

The hollow feelings she'd carried inside her all through her time in D.C. now had names. Desolation, fear, sorrow—all because she was losing the love of her life to divorce. But she'd almost lost him to death. No chance then of healing conversations, of sexual healing.

The sharp knock at the bathroom door made her jump. Lotion squirted onto the mirror.

"Yes?"

"Melinda, you have a visitor."

She opened the door a crack. Why not give Nick a little sneak preview?

"Who is it?" She looked into his eyes. Tried to. But his face was set in stone, his eyes guarded like a watchdog's.

"The senator."

The air in the living room crackled with tension.

Senator Hodges looked out of place in his Brooks Brothers suit and overcoat, his cell phone handy in his lambskin gloves.

"Melinda, I'm so sorry to bother you at home." He walked over to kiss her cheek.

"No problem." What had possessed him to come here in person?

"I've found out about an award that hasn't been handled properly at the office."

And he'd come here to chew her out on a holiday?

She couldn't think of one instance of his taking personal time to handle staff business, ever.

The doorbell rang and all three heads turned.

"Now what?" Nick left the room with no other comment. He'd never felt comfortable around the "muckety-mucks," as he referred to politicians and CEO types. The only leaders he respected were his military commanders.

Melinda heard his exclamation of surprise and went to see who was at the door.

A petite brunette woman and three children, none taller than Nick's chest, embraced Nick in a hug.

"Nick?"

Melinda could tell that her voice sounded frail.

Nick pulled away from the crowd and turned toward her.

"Melinda, I'd like you to meet Margarite Sanson and her children, Mikey, Peter and Haley."

"Hi."

The young mother held out her hand.

"It's so nice to meet you. I'm sorry about the intrusion, but the kids and I had to be here."

"No problem. Nick?"

"This is Mrs. *Tommy* Sanson." His voice was quiet and purposeful.

Shock jolted Melinda out of her confusion.

Tommy—Nick's comrade in arms. The one killed by the IED.

Melinda looked into the mirror of "it could have been me" as she reached out her hand to Margarite.

"I'm so very sorry about your husband."

"We are, too." Margarite's eyes were shadowed but Melinda saw the strength in them. "Each day gets a tiny bit better, though." Margarite hugged her children to her. "Right, kids?"

Quiet murmurs were the only response.

"Come on into the living room, everyone." Senator Hodge's voice boomed from the family room. He wasn't a patient man, and today was no exception.

Once they were all assembled in front of the fireplace, Senator Hodges went into political-presenter mode.

"I'm sorry to interrupt everyone's Thanksgiving celebration. But, be that as it may, it is indeed a day for thanksgiving. I've come here today to present you, Nick, with the Purple Heart that you refused while you were in the hospital."

Nick's face resembled the white-washed wall behind him.

"Sir—"

Senator Hodges held up his right hand.

"No 'buts,' Nick. You've earned this. But today isn't just about you."

He turned to Tommy's family.

"I am truly sorry for your loss. I am, and the entire country is. I asked you to drive here today to give Nick the same award Tommy earned. The same award Tommy would give Nick if he could be here to do so."

Senator Hodges reached into his briefcase and produced a small hinged box. He presented it to Margarite. She opened it with her children looking on.

Margarite looked at the medal, then up at Nick.

Tears ran down her cheeks. Melinda's own tears needed no further prompting.

"Mommy, why is it purple?"

"It's the color for brave heroes, sweetheart, and your daddy was one. So is Mr. Nick."

Nick remained silent, and Melinda thought his teeth would crack from how tightly he clenched them. She longed to move next to him, to soothe him, but this was his moment.

His and Tommy's.

"Margarite?" Senator Hodges prompted.

Margarite took hold of her oldest child, Mikey, and handed him the medal. She whispered in his ear.

Mikey glanced at his mom for final approval. She nodded and gently pushed his shoulder, nudging him toward Nick.

The boy straightened, then walked over to Nick.

"Sir, please accept this for my daddy. He loved you a lot and…and my family loves you."

What else could Nick do?

He accepted the award, and his rightful place in his nation's history.

The door closed behind the Sansons, who'd stayed for a while after the senator left, before Margarite said they had to be going, as her parents were expecting them for dinner at noon. She lived three hours away, in Syracuse.

Nick turned to Melinda and there was no question about what was on his mind.

"Come," he issued the command softly. Melinda placed her hand in his and followed him back to the bedroom.

Their bedroom.

They hadn't been together since a few months before he'd left. The second time.

Even though they'd been heading toward their break-up for almost a year before that, they hadn't always been able to keep their hands off of each other.

Their physical attraction had grown deeper over the years. It often took only a simple glance or caress, and Melinda was ready, willing and eager to go to bed with Nick.

She knew what today meant, though. This wasn't going to be the last fling before their divorce.

There wasn't going to be a divorce.

"Nick, are we—"

"Yes."

As he answered her, he was undressing her, kissing each area as he exposed it. In three more kisses she'd be naked and incapable of intelligible speech.

He eased them both onto the bed.

"Don't stop." She grasped his shoulders as he kissed her belly, then moved down to her hips and started pressing kisses through her panties.

"I won't, darling." His kisses were urgent, his breath hot. Perhaps this was what the problem had been all along—they hadn't had enough sex.

A giggle escaped her.

"Nick." Her laughter became a moan that he wrenched from her with one quick stroke of his tongue. Before she lost her mind to desire, Nick leaned on his elbow and cradled her face in his hands.

"This isn't 'one last time,' Melinda. This is our new beginning. Deal?"

"Deal." She pulled his head to hers.

"Who do we tell first?" Melinda stroked Nick's chest. It was nearly two o'clock. Aunt Lille was expecting them in an hour, and they had to pick up Grandpa Jack on the way.

"Jack."

"I think he'll figure it out over the mashed potatoes."

Nick grunted. A sexy, low-pitched grunt.

"I can't wait to tell Aunt Lille."

"Melinda, you have to tell Jack first. We both do." She pushed up on her elbow, her breast brushing his arm.

"Okay. But why are you so intense about it?"

Nick kissed her full on the lips.

"Let's get dressed and I'll fill you in on the way there, okay?"

"Sure," she murmured against his mouth.

* * *

As they drove the short three miles to Jack's, Nick told Melinda about Jack's cancer.

"Oh, my God. No wonder he wouldn't let me come back until I finished reading the journals. He knew he couldn't keep it from me…."

"I think he's probably past the point of caring about that, Melinda. But he wants you to get through the journals so you can ask any questions while he's still here. I think he figures that each day could be his last."

"You said he looked well yesterday!" Her voice reflected her shock.

"He did. Better than the past few times I've seen him. But he's also had Janice coming around."

"Janice." She'd been Grammy's nurse. "It's that bad already?"

"Remember, he's been dealing with it for a couple of years now. It's probably a miracle he's lived this long."

Nick pulled into Jack's driveway and turned off the engine. He faced Melinda.

"Look, I know he's your grandfather, and this is your show. But one suggestion—let him lead any talk about his illness, okay?"

Melinda offered him a weak smile through her tears.

Grandpa Jack didn't immediately answer the door, and Melinda's heart raced in anxiety. When Janice opened the door, she was alarmed.

"Janice, is he okay?"

"Yes, yes, he's just resting after a full morning of cartoons." Grandpa Jack had always loved watching Saturday-morning cartoons with Melinda as she grew up. Now that cartoons were available twenty-four hours a day, Jack could be found watching them at any time.

"I wish I'd watched them with him." Melinda choked back a sob. Nick put his hand on her shoulder when they were all inside the kitchen.

"It's okay, honey. He's still here, and he needs your understanding and strength right now."

"Okay." Melinda drew in a deep breath. Grandpa Jack didn't need her tears.

Janice put her hand on Melinda's arm. "Why don't you two have a cup of coffee while you wait. When Jack wakes up, you can talk to him. He's all excited about going to Lille's today."

"Thanks, Janice. As always, you're an angel."

She looked at Nick. "Will you call Aunt Lille and tell her we'll get there when we get there?"

"Done." While Nick pulled out his cell phone, Melinda went in to sit with Grandpa Jack.

Two cups of coffee later, Jack stirred from his nap. Melinda noticed the drained quality in his expression. Nick was right; Grandpa Jack had been fighting his own illness for a long time.

He blinked open his eyes and through their swollen lids Melinda glimpsed his violet-blue irises. Tired and old, but they still had the spark that belonged only to Grandpa Jack.

"Hey, Grandpa Jack." She squeezed his hand.

"Hey, yourself, kiddo." He smiled at her.

"Are you ready for a cup of coffee?"

"Sure."

Janice maneuvered the hospital bed into position and adjusted Jack's blankets and pillows while Melinda returned to the kitchen to get his coffee. Nick followed her.

"Just the way you like it, Grandpa." Melinda placed the familiar mug in his hands. Hands that had fought through a war, hugged her, cultivated a garden. Their withered state clawed at her stomach, and her heart wept for the loss of his strength.

"Thanks, sweetheart. I see you brought your better half." He grinned at Nick.

Nick rubbed Jack's shoulder. "Hey, Jack."

"You told her, didn't you?"

"That I'm the bionic man? Sure." Nick kept his tone light, joking.

Jack waved his hand in dismissal.

"That's not the big news I'm talking about."

"It's okay, Grandpa." She didn't want him to have to spell it out for her. The fact that he was dying was enough of a burden. For all of them.

"Melinda, it *is* okay. I'm on my way to be with Esmée. One last journey."

"Oh, Grandpa." Melinda couldn't stem the tears that spilled down her cheeks.

"So you've finished the books?" Clearly Grandpa Jack didn't want to focus on his illness.

"Yes, yes, I did. Yesterday. I'll never be able to thank you enough for trusting me with them, Grandpa Jack." She gave him a tremulous smile.

"Glad you're still willing to see me after learning all my secrets." He winked a swollen eye at her.

"Grandpa, I don't know how you and Grammy made it through all you did. You're both heroes, saints, I don't know, *wonderful!*"

"Nonsense. We just did what we had to. You'd do the same. But Grammy wanted you to know that you came into the world loved, with a family who was always ready and willing to fight for you."

"I know that, Grandpa."

"Do you have any questions?"

Melinda looked at the aged face of the man who'd been a father, grandfather and now war hero to her. Hell yes, she had questions. But none he needed to answer, none that would make a difference after he passed.

"Just one, Grandpa."

"Shoot."

"What was that necklace you gave Grammy at her eightieth birthday party all about?"

"The Whitley? Why, that was the aircraft I dropped out of into Belgium. Esmée always said the angels brought me to her. So I had a copy of the actual angel that did the deed."

Jack chuckled. "Your aunt Lille has the necklace

now. She'll pass it on to her girls. You're not jealous, are you?"

"Jealous? No, no, Grandpa Jack. There's nothing I want from you or Grammy other than what you've already given me."

"What's that, Melinda?"

"My life."

Epilogue

Melinda's Journal

August 15, 2008

The sun shines so bright outside my window. Essie is nursing and looks like a cherub. I can't believe it's already been a month since she arrived.

Who would've thought it—all Nick and I needed to conceive was some time together without either of us obsessing about work or our relationship.

I'm a mommy at forty-one!

I miss Grandpa Jack and wish he could've seen Essie. He died the week before we found out I was pregnant.

She has his ears and his feet. He missed her by nine months. I was so sure she'd be a boy! But no, it was my beautiful Esmée. Pink, plump and perfect.

My words will never be as fluid as Grammy's were. One day, Essie will read this and she'll see who the real writer in the family was. Her great-grandmother. Her namesake.

I can smell the coffee Nick's brewing. What will he surprise me with for breakfast today? He needs to get back to work, but he's assured me the manager he hired last month has things under control. But I think about the orders he has pending—for fifty-three gardens!

Nick. My angel, my savior. I almost lost him. But I thank God I found him—we found each other—again. It's better than it ever was. Better than it ever could've been between us without everything we've been through.

And all because of you, Grammy. I know somehow you're reading this as I write it. Or you hear my thoughts. You helped send me Essie, and that's why I've named her after you.

You were one of a kind, Grammy. So were you, Grandpa Jack. I miss you both and I'll never stop loving you.

SPECIAL EDITION®

Life, Love and Family

*These contemporary romances will strike a chord
with you as heroines juggle life
and relationships on their way to true love.*

New York Times *bestselling author Linda Lael Miller
brings you a BRAND-NEW contemporary story
featuring her fan-favorite McKettrick family.*

Meg McKettrick is surprised to be reunited with
her high-school flame, Brad O'Ballivan. After
enjoying a career as a country-and-western singer,
Brad aches for a home and family...and seeing
Meg again makes him realize he still loves her. But
their pride manages to interfere with love...until
an unexpected matchmaker gets involved.

*Turn the page for a sneak preview of
THE McKETTRICK WAY
by Linda Lael Miller*

*On sale November 20,
wherever books are sold.*

Brad shoved the truck into gear and drove to the bottom of the hill, where the road forked. Turn left, and he'd be home in five minutes. Turn right, and he was headed for Indian Rock.

He had no damn business going to Indian Rock.

He had nothing to say to Meg McKettrick, and if he never set eyes on the woman again, it would be two weeks too soon.

He turned right.

He couldn't have said why.

He just drove straight to the Dixie Dog Drive-In.

Back in the day, he and Meg used to meet at the Dixie Dog, by tacit agreement, when either of them had been away. It had been some kind of universe thing, purely intuitive.

Passing familiar landmarks, Brad told himself he ought to turn around. The old days were gone. Things had ended badly between him and Meg anyhow, and she wasn't going to be at the Dixie Dog.

He kept driving.

He rounded a bend, and there was the Dixie Dog. Its big neon sign, a giant hot dog, was all lit up and going through its corny sequence—first it was covered in red squiggles of light, meant to suggest ketchup, and then yellow, for mustard.

Brad pulled into one of the slots next to a speaker, rolled down the truck window and ordered.

A girl roller-skated out with the order about five minutes later.

When she wheeled up to the driver's window, smiling, her eyes went wide with recognition and she dropped the tray with a clatter.

Silently Brad swore. Damn if he hadn't forgotten he was a famous country singer.

The girl, a skinny thing wearing too much eye makeup, immediately started to cry. "I'm sorry!" she sobbed, squatting to gather up the mess.

"It's okay," Brad answered quietly, leaning to look down at her, catching a glimpse of her plastic name tag. "It's okay, Mandy. No harm done."

"I'll get you another dog and a shake right away, Mr. O'Ballivan!"

"Mandy?"

She stared up at him pitifully, sniffling. Thanks to the copious tears, most of the goop on her eyes had slid south. "Yes?"

"When you go back inside, could you not mention seeing me?"

"But you're Brad O'Ballivan!"

"Yeah," he answered, suppressing a sigh. "I know."

She rolled a little closer. "You wouldn't happen to have a picture you could autograph for me, would you?"

"Not with me," Brad answered.

"You could sign this napkin, though," Mandy said. "It's only got a little chocolate on the corner."

Brad took the paper napkin and her order pen, and scrawled his name. Handed both items back through the window.

She turned and whizzed back toward the side entrance to the Dixie Dog.

Brad waited, marveling that he hadn't considered incidents like this one before he'd decided to come back home. In retrospect, it seemed shortsighted, to say the least, but the truth was, he'd expected to be—Brad O'Ballivan.

Presently Mandy skated back out again, and this time she managed to hold on to the tray.

"I didn't tell a soul!" she whispered. "But Heather and Darlene *both* asked me why my mascara was all smeared." Efficiently she hooked the tray onto the bottom edge of the window.

Brad extended payment, but Mandy shook her head.

"The boss said it's on the house, since I dumped your first order on the ground."

He smiled. "Okay, then. Thanks."

Mandy retreated, and Brad was just reaching for the food when a bright red Blazer whipped into the space beside his. The driver's door sprang open, crashing into the metal speaker, and somebody got out in a hurry.

Something quickened inside Brad.

And in the next moment Meg McKettrick was standing practically on his running board, her blue eyes blazing.

Brad grinned. "I guess you're not over me after all," he said.

REQUEST YOUR FREE BOOKS!

2 FREE NOVELS PLUS 2 FREE GIFTS!

 HARLEQUIN®

E V E R L A S T I N G   L O V E ™

Every great love has a story to tell ™

YES! Please send me 2 FREE Harlequin® Everlasting Love™ novels and my 2 FREE gifts. After receiving them, if I don't wish to receive any more books, I can return the shipping statement marked "cancel." If I don't cancel, I will receive 4 brand-new novels every other month and be billed just $4.47 per book in the U.S. or $4.99 per book in Canada, plus 25¢ shipping and handling per book and applicable taxes, if any*. That's a savings of about 15% off the cover price! I understand that accepting the 2 free books and gifts places me under no obligation to buy anything. I can always return a shipment and cancel at any time. Even if I never buy another book from Harlequin, the two free books and gifts are mine to keep forever.

153 HDN ELX4   353 HDN ELYG

Name	(PLEASE PRINT)	
Address		Apt.
City	State/Prov.	Zip/Postal Code

Signature (if under 18, a parent or guardian must sign)

Mail to the **Harlequin Reader Service®:**
IN U.S.A.: P.O. Box 1867, Buffalo, NY 14240-1867
IN CANADA: P.O. Box 609, Fort Erie, Ontario L2A 5X3

Not valid to current Harlequin Everlasting Love subscribers.

Want to try two free books from another line?
Call 1-800-873-8635 or visit www.morefreebooks.com.

* Terms and prices subject to change without notice. NY residents add applicable sales tax. Canadian residents will be charged applicable provincial taxes and GST. This offer is limited to one order per household. All orders subject to approval. Credit or debit balances in a customer's account(s) may be offset by any other outstanding balance owed by or to the customer. Please allow 4 to 6 weeks for delivery.

Your Privacy: Harlequin is committed to protecting your privacy. Our Privacy Policy is available online at www.eHarlequin.com or upon request from the Reader Service. From time to time we make our lists of customers available to reputable firms who may have a product or service of interest to you. If you would prefer we not share your name and address, please check here. ☐

HEL07

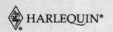

EVERLASTING LOVE™

Every great love has a story to tell™

Martin Collins was the man
Keti Whitechapen had always loved but
just couldn't marry. But one Christmas Eve
Keti finds a dog she names Marley.
That night she has a dream about
Christmas past. And Christmas present—
and future. A future that could include the
man she's continued to love.

Look for

A Spirit of Christmas

by

Margot Early

Available December wherever you buy books.

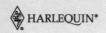

EVERLASTING LOVE™

Every great love has a story to tell™

COMING NEXT MONTH

#21 CHRISTMAS PRESENTS AND PAST
by Janice Kay Johnson

My true love gave to me... Every Christmas gift Will and Dinah exchange is a symbol of their love. The tradition begins on their very first date, when Will arrives with an exquisitely wrapped present, and it continues every holiday season thereafter—whether they're together or apart—until something in their lives goes very wrong. And then only an unexpected gift can make things right.

#22 A SPIRIT OF CHRISTMAS by Margot Early

A modern retelling of Dickens's *A Christmas Carol*. It is said that Keti and Martin Collins keep Christmas very well. But it wasn't always this way.... Despite—or perhaps because of—Martin Collins, the man she's always loved but couldn't marry, Keti Whitechapel had a "Bah, humbug" attitude toward life. But one Christmas Eve, Keti finds a dog she names Marley. That night she has a dream about Christmas past. And Christmas present—and future. A future that could include the man she's loved all these years...

www.eHarlequin.com

HECNM1107